ELEMENTAL BLADE

THE CURSED BLADE SERIES

BOOK 2

M.P. STARKWEATHER

CONTENTS

Author's Note

Welcome back to The Cursed Blade Series!

Please be aware of content warnings for this story.

This story contains an assassin's guild, a witch who can control elements, graphic murder, discussion of sexual assault, discussion of drugging, shifters, warlocks, shadow wielders, Fae, a psychic, people being kidnapped and murdered for their powers, and detailed, graphic sexual situations.

Your mental health is important, so please be aware of the content warnings as you begin.

I want to dedicate this book to my two biggest fans, my husband Josh and my son Thom, who will probably never read any of my books. Thanks for pushing me to chase my dream. I love you both to the moon and back.

PROLOGUE

TWENTY YEARS AGO

AMARA

"Are you sure?" I ask my best friend as she presses her infant against my chest. "Mirela, this isn't something you can change your mind about tomorrow."

Mirela looks at me with haunted pale blue eyes. As tears spill down her cheeks, she nods. "I am too weak to protect her, and you know what the prophecy says. You and Raj will keep her safe. You have to."

I wrap my arms around the closest thing to a sister I've ever had. I'm humbled that she trusts me with this. "We won't let you down," I assure her. She nods and lays back against the bed again. I know she's exhausted and needs to rest.

"Now go; hurry," she insists as an explosion sounds somewhere behind the tent where she gave birth only minutes ago. Nodding, I press the baby tighter to my chest and duck outside.

Raj and I lock eyes for a moment and his go wide with realization. "No, Amara, we can't," he starts.

"I tried to talk her out of it, but Mirela insisted. What was I supposed to do? Raj, love, we have to take the baby somewhere safe and protect her until the time of the prophecy." Without waiting for his response, I turn and race back to our home. There isn't time to pack; the attacks have begun.

Once inside our own tent, Raj grabs a backpack and quickly tosses in what we'll need to get away. I want to help, but the baby is crying and I can't let her draw them to us. My focus has to be on keeping her calm. I know that Mirela will do everything in her power to distract those chasing us.

I have no doubt that this decision will cost us all our lives before it's done. I just hope we have enough time to teach the little one. With our bag strapped to his back, Raj helps me swaddle the child and tuck her carefully into a wrap so my hands are free to protect us if needed. There is so much I want to say, even to Mirela, but there is no time. We have to run if we want to live.

Raj leads us through the dense forest. I don't know where we'll go...it's not like we have a car or family outside the village. My love and I are on our own now. How are we going to survive and care for this child?

I don't have time to worry about anything except keeping up with Raj. He moves so quickly, even without shifting into his wolf form. When Raj stops short in front of me, I barely miss slamming into his back. Before I can ask what's wrong, a circle of blue flame surrounds us.

"Give us the child," a voice booms. I turn in a circle, searching the mix of darkness and flame for the source. Raj jerks his head to the left, and I lock onto what he's staring at. I love this man and his enhanced wolf senses.

A bolt of lightning streaks from my fingertips to the figure hiding in the trees. His scream rings out as he falls to the ground, incinerated. As soon as he's taken care of, the blue flames disappear, and we continue running.

RAJ

I know the details of the prophecy, and there is no doubt that this child is the one. That doesn't mean I'm excited about the prospect of losing my life or my love to ensure that this plays out correctly. I know that Amara won't give up. Her stubborn determination is one of the things I love most about her.

So, once the immediate danger is handled, I follow Amara through the winding trees and into the edge of the city. This is not a place where we spend a lot of time. It's crowded, noisy, and smells like a mixture of sewage and smoke. My wolf senses are overwhelmed by it all, and I fight the desire to return to the forest.

It's not safe for the child there, so I have to push forward. I was not the one who made the promise, but I will do everything I can to keep my mate's word to her best friend. Mirela was the closest thing to a sister my woman ever had. I loved and respected her for the way she cared for my Amara.

That doesn't mean I have to be happy about being forced into the city. I refuse to take my misery out on my mate, especially when she's protecting our future.

"Amara, wait," I say quietly as we enter the outskirts of the city. She pauses and looks over her shoulder at me. "There's a hidden cache with emergency money and identification not far from here. If we're going to hide out, we'll need the money at least."

She nods, cradling the infant to her chest. I don't know what we'll do about the baby, but perhaps we won't have to prove her lineage just yet. I need some time to reconnect with my city contacts. Then we'll have exactly what we need.

Amara follows me to the tree with the hidden compartment and waits while I open it and clear out the cache. I stuff everything into my backpack, and we continue into the city. My love's powers assist us in persuading a landlord to rent an apartment to us, even with our limited money, and lack of jobs.

Within a week, we are settled in, living in the middle of the city. The apartment is small, but functional. There's a park nearby that will give the little one a place to learn about her powers. We'll have to teach her to protect herself. I just hope that she actually gets to have a childhood, too.

"Did Mirela tell you the baby's name?" I ask, tucking the little one into bed.

"Her name is Zola."

Dark Desires

PRESENT DAY

ZOLA

Relief washes over me when I realize that Amara and Raj aren't following me. As much as I want to be a regular college student, I know that I'm different. Not only because of my powers. Being able to control the elements is a thrilling feeling.

But the past year, I've had these urges that I can't explain or discuss with my guardians.

Part of me wishes my mother was still around. Maybe she would understand. Or maybe I'm just a monster. Does it matter that I don't let myself lose control unless it's around someone who deserves it? Of course, the argument could be made that no one deserves the things I've done. All I really know is that I'm protecting people from being hurt, and that neither Raj nor Amara would understand or approve of my methods. And I know exactly how much of my power I can use before one of them is alerted. I just have to keep everything below that threshold, and I'll be fine.

My heart thumps as I follow the frat boy I've been tracking around the corner into a dark alley. I pull my hood over my head, tucking my hair away to hide my identity. Does John know I've been watching him for the past month? I don't think so. The bastard has been too busy drugging and raping girls who can't even remember what happened to them. If I get my way, he'll no longer be an issue after today. I just have to get him alone. And this dark alley may be the exact place to do it. *What the fuck is he doing here anyway?*

I don't have time to ponder his reasons, before he turns and calls out to me. Well, shit. I hadn't meant for him to see me, but it doesn't matter. Dead men can't turn murderers in, now, can they? A smirk plays across my face at his confusion.

"Why are you following me?" he asks, hands balled into fists at his sides.

"Are you scared, John?" I ask in return, tilting my head to the side as I feel my power surge inside me. Moisture tingles in the air, the hair on my arms rises at the chill flowing through me. "Because you should be."

His annoyance morphs into anger, scrunching his face and turning it red. "I'm not scared of you. Why would I be? You don't even have a weapon. What do you want?" he snarls.

"Bold of you to assume that you have *anything* I would be interested in, John," I answer.

"How do you know my name? Why are you following me?" He fumbles with something, and I realize that he's pulling out his phone. Oh, well. That won't be an issue.

I stare at the small black rectangle, narrowing my eyes to focus my power. Smoke rolls from the speaker, and John drops the device. "Fuck! How did you do that?" His eyes go wide with the accusation. My smirk grows, and I chuckle. This is way more fun than the last one. I should probably see a therapist about this, but I don't have time for that concern right now. I have to kill a rapist.

"Oh, John. You poor boy. Do you really not have any idea what we're doing here?" I ask, tilting my head to the opposite side. "You're going to get what you deserve for what you've done."

"I haven't done anything. What are you talking about?" His words claim innocence, but his eyes are filled with fear. He knows exactly why I'm here.

"Don't play dumb, John. You know what you did. As many times as you've done it, if you forget that easily, there's something even more wrong with you than whatever makes you think it's okay to treat women that way," I say, pausing when I notice that he's backing away from me. Well, that won't do.

I turn my power toward his feet, melting the asphalt under them, then sending a breeze to cool it back down once his sneakers are stuck. That'll keep him from running. Surprise and protest spill out of his mouth, but I'm not listening. He tugs at his feet, trying to get them out of the shoes effectively imbedded in the alley.

"Now, now, John. Katy deserves justice, doesn't she?" His eyes go wide at the mention of one of his victims. "And what about Amy? Sarah? Jenny? How many others were there, John?"

The frat boy sputters and stammers in response, no actual words coming from him.

I glare at him, and something about it shuts him up. "How many women did you drug and rape, John?" Understanding washes over him, and I see the moment he realizes exactly why I'm here. "You know what? Don't answer that. It'll just piss me off more than I already am, and it's not like you're gonna live to do it again."

"Wait! You can't kill me," he insists.

"And just why not?" I ask with a laugh. It's obvious to both of us that I am more than capable of detaining him, and I know just how easy it would be to drown him in this alley, even with no body of water nearby.

"My family has money. I can pay you. They'll pay you. Just like those girls," he offers.

"So, you gaslight them into believing that they were willing participants, then pay them off so they have an abortion if needed, and you get off scot-free? That's not nice, John. But thank you for offering me your money. I have no need of it, though. What I do need, is for you to die," I answer.

"P-please," he begs, dropping to his knees awkwardly since his feet are still stuck.

"Please, what, John?" I ask, barely hiding the amusement that elates me. My heart races as I prepare for the endorphin rush that will follow using my power to take his life.

"Please, don't." Tears stream down his face. It's clear that he understands I'm serious. He knows that he's about to die.

"And just how well did that work for your *victims*, John? Did you stop when they asked you to? When they begged you not to rape them?"

His expression is enough of an answer, and I can tell that he still doesn't think he did anything wrong. "Why do you care? Those bitches led me on, then tried to ignore me. I only took what they originally offered. I didn't rape them."

"I've seen police reports that disagree with that, John. I'm tired of this conversation. It's time to end this. I have better things to spend my time on than trash like you," I say, turning my back on him and walking away.

"You can't leave me here like this," he growls. "I will find you when I get free, and you'll regret this."

I stop, a smile spreading across my face. This. This is the monster I was hunting. The one who will escalate to murder if he's not stopped. I would know, given my current hobbies. Without a word, I turn back to face him, my smile never falter-ing. Instead of stepping closer, I lift one hand, pointing it at his chest. The beauty of my powers is that I don't have to be close for them to work. I only have to connect with the elements.

Reaching inside his chest with my abilities, I pull the water from his blood, forming it into a fist wrapped around his heart. I know from my research that this will look like he had a heart attack. There will be no evidence that anyone else was involved. Once the police decide that, there will be no investigation. This isn't my first kill, but the thrill races through me just the same.

Sometimes I wonder if simply killing the monsters will remain enough for me. I've studied serial killers in one of my psych classes, and I know all about escalation. Essentially, I'm one of them, and I know it. Will there come a time when I want to kill and find out if I can get away with it without the use of my powers? I have no idea. Distraction is not something I need right now, so I push those thoughts away as I end John's miserable life.

When his body slumps to the ground, I remember to release his feet and smooth out the asphalt as if he'd never been stuck there. I stand there a minute too long, staring at his body, when someone rounds the corner into the alley and sees us.

"Hey, is everything okay?" the man asks.

Shit. I can't get caught now. I turn so I'm angled away from him slightly. "I don't know. I was walking through, and this guy was just laying here," I respond in a deeper voice than my usual one. With any luck, the man will think I'm just another college guy cutting through the alley to get back to campus.

"I'll call 9-1-1," he says, and I nod, watching as he turns away from the scene, as if he's looking for help, and pulls out his phone. The moment his eyes are no longer on me, I run down the alley, ducking around the corner and disappearing into the crowd that's heading back to campus. My heart races, and I wonder if this is what John felt before I killed him.

A horn blares, and I freeze, realizing I'm in the middle of the street. Sure, I'm in the crosswalk, but that doesn't really matter when the crossing light is red. The yellow and black checkered car barrels toward me, and I know they aren't going to have time to stop. There's no way for me to dive out of the way, either. I hear a scream, and everything stops.

That scream is coming from me. And when I say everything stops, I mean everything. Cars, people, birds flying above the streets. Everything is frozen in place, covered in an almost imperceptible layer of ice. I don't know how this happened. What I do know, is that I am going to be in deep shit with Raj and Amara over it. Fuck. I'm not sure how to undo it, so instead, I race home.

My guardians have spent the last fifteen years lecturing me about keeping my powers hidden. They've explained that some unknown force is after me, and it's not safe. I have no proof of it, but I feel something dark following me, so I'm pretty sure that they were telling the truth. Shit. I have to get home.

Rushing up the stairs of our building, I pause for a moment outside the door to the apartment I've called home for as long as I can remember. My breaths come in gasps. It takes a moment to calm my racing heart and loosen the vice around my lungs.

I push the door open, determined to pretend nothing just happened, while checking to make sure my guardians are okay. That ominous feeling in my chest increases until I feel as if an elephant is sitting on me. Something is wrong. At this time of day, Raj should be sitting on the couch watching TV while Amara is cooking dinner.

The number of times that pattern has differed can be counted on one hand. And that's over the last twenty years. My guardians are creatures of habit, and each habit was carefully created to keep me safe. I can't help thinking that if something has happened to them, it's my fault.

Of course, it's my fault. They told me how dangerous it was to use my powers. But did I listen? No, of course not. I felt like I knew my own powers better than they could. And now I'm worried that I may have been wrong. Normally, that wouldn't be a big deal. I cannot shake the feeling that this situation is not normal, though.

I walk through the apartment slowly, terror gripping my heart. There is no sign of either of my caretakers. I wouldn't normally enter their private space without permission, but I'm worried. Pushing away the sense of dread at what I might find, I open the door to their bedroom.

Blood runs down the walls, pooling in the corners of the room. No, it can't be. There's too much blood. I can't force myself to cross the threshold. Scanning the scene, my eyes catch on a gooey pile in the middle of the floor before finding another on the bed. Bile rises in my throat. I turn and race to the bathroom, barely making it before I get sick. Once the vomiting slows to dry heaving, I wash my face and look into the mirror.

The realization that I'm on my own starts to settle in. I can't stay here. If whatever killed them comes back—it's not safe.

I dash to my bedroom, grabbing my backpack on the way. I empty it on the floor, knowing I won't need the books or school supplies anymore. There's no way to return to my normal life after this. Understanding that, I make sure to leave my cell phone behind as well. I can't risk someone using it to track me.

Careful consideration and even more mindful packing fill my backpack with what I'll need to survive for a few days. As I head to the door, I notice Amara's purse on the table. Stealing is wrong, but is it stealing if the owner is dead? I'm conflicted, but that doesn't stop me from taking her cash and searching for Raj's wallet. Once I've scrounged up all the money in the apartment, I briefly debate taking a knife from the kitchen.

Shaking my head at the ridiculous idea, I wipe away the tears that started to fall as I ransacked my home. I don't need weapons. I am a weapon. It no longer matters that they would be disappointed in my choices. Amara and Raj are gone, and I have to protect myself. With nowhere to go, and no clear plan, I drop my keys inside the door before closing it behind me. Perhaps I'll get lucky and whoever finds them will think I've been killed too. Otherwise, I'll have these monsters hunting me as well as the police.

I know better than to think I won't be a suspect. We've watched enough true crime shows to understand that the police usually look at whoever is closest to the victim first. And who would be closer to Raj and Amara than me? No one. At this point, I'm better off if everyone thinks I'm dead too.

The thought spurs me to reenter the apartment. It won't take much to make it convincing. And it's not like there's anything here with my DNA on it. I doubt they'd go further than a visual inspection. But just in case...

Staring at what remains of my guardians, I use my powers, the abilities to control water and air, to move a bit of one pile and a bit of the other. I create a third lump between them, then grab a knife from the kitchen. One small cut on my palm, and I direct the blood to mix with the new glob on the floor. Making sure not to drop any, I clean the knife, and bandage my hand, dropping a few emergency medical supplies in my bag.

With the hope that it's enough, I once again say goodbye to the couple who raised me. Guilt tears at my heart as I walk away. I have no idea where I'll go or who I'm even hiding from. They never explained that part. All I can do is hope that I can hide well enough.

I pull my hood up again to cover my dark hair. Tears start to fall again as I walk away from the only home I've ever known. I have to stay alive, otherwise, Raj and Amara sacrificed their lives for nothing. From their stories, I know there's some prophecy about my powers, and that it's rare for someone from our home to have control of all four elements. But I have no idea who is after me, or how to protect myself from them.

Being an elemental witch in the city is definitely a challenge. Maybe that will work in my favor. Whoever is hunting me will expect to find me near nature, so logically, all I have to do is stay as far away from the local parks as I can. I'll have to visit at some point to recharge my power, but I can manage a few days in the dark.

I head toward the docks, knowing that there are abandoned warehouses and shipping containers in that area. It shouldn't be hard to find places to hide where I can move around daily and not be noticed. If anyone sees me, they'll assume I'm just some homeless person, and ignore me. It's what our society does.

Once I'm inside a warehouse, I climb the stairs to the top floor. Moving silently, thanks to my powers, I search the top floor until I find an office with a bathroom connected. This will do for tonight. I can use my powers for everything I need, and no one will know I was here.

I settle down in the corner of the office, near the bathroom and a window. The sun is going down, but I still have to be careful not to be seen from outside. I can't imagine anyone would be watching this building. That doesn't mean I'm willing to take unnecessary risks.

Without my phone, I have no way to tell what time it is. I pull my brush out of my bag and quickly braid my hair. The temperature starts to drop, so I drag my hood back up and rest my head on my bag, falling into a fitful sleep.

LAYING LOW

ZOLA

A NOISE JERKS ME awake. I sit up with a gasp, blinking to clear my vision. Something is wrong, but everything looks just like it did when I drifted off. Hair on the back of my neck stands up, and I know I'm sensing danger. Is it a shift in the air that's warning me? Or a change in the moisture? I can't be sure, because I haven't used my powers for anything but getting justice for girls at school who'd been violated. And it's not like I've done that a lot.

With no idea who's hunting me, or how to protect myself from them, I can't afford to stay and fight. I have to run. My thoughts focus on survival, and I quickly get to my feet. I secure my hood over my dark hair, then pull on my backpack. In this moment, I feel both older and younger than my actual age. My mind starts to wonder how things would have been different if I'd been able to stay with my parents.

I can't let myself go down that rabbit hole, though. Shaking my head to clear those thoughts, I stand up and creep toward the door. Getting out of here without being seen is going to be a challenge, since there are only two ways out. I chose this place to hide because there were limited ways someone could surprise me. Now I regret that choice. It may have been better to hide somewhere that was easier to escape.

I silently push the door to the north stairwell open, using a tiny bit of magic to ensure that it doesn't make a sound when it opens or closes. After a brief pause to listen at the top of the stairs, I run down the stairs as quietly as I can. I know that tapping into my magic will make me more of a target, and I want to avoid that if I can.

Footsteps echo up the stairwell, and I stop on the third-floor landing to listen. Shit, they're getting closer. Did I go the wrong way? Or are there more of them than I thought? It doesn't matter either way, I have to find another way out of here.

The door clicks shut quietly behind me as I dart across the open area on this floor. If I had more time, I might stop to wonder what they're putting in this building. As it stands, I barely have time to stop and listen at the opposite stairwell door before pushing through it and running down the last three flights of stairs.

Once I'm outside, I see a Hummer and a Jeep parked in front of the building. Luckily, whoever they belong to didn't leave anyone to watch them. As much as I would love to borrow one, I know it's a bad idea. Unless my goal is to get caught, and if that's the case, I should just turn around and walk back inside. I don't know a lot about the people who want me, but I know enough that I can't turn myself in. Amara and Raj gave their lives to protect me. And I will not disrespect them like that.

Adrenaline carries me past the first row of shipping containers. I need a place to hide until I'm sure it's safe to move again. Movement nearby has me ducking into a small shack between containers. I lean against the door, listening, as boots stomp past. The windows are dark, and I wonder if that's just dirt, or if they're actually tinted. That's not really important right now, so I settle down on the floor against the door. I can't afford to move right now, because I have no idea if those guys are coming back or not.

I close my eyes and focus on regulating my breathing. A panic attack will not help right now. It's been so long since I've had one, that I nearly miss the signs. When I was a child, I had plenty of panic attacks while I was learning to control and suppress my magic.

I wish I'd learned how to actually use it, but I understand how risky that would have been for all three of us. Guilt wraps cold fingers around my heart, squeezing until I can't hold back the tears. Raj and Amara are dead because of me. It's my fault. If I had only waited longer to hunt John down, maybe things would have been different.

Letting those thoughts control me isn't helpful. I know they'll only lead to me getting caught. Angry voices accompany boot thumps, and I flatten myself against the base of the door. Hopefully, if I can't see them, they won't be able to see me. From my new vantage point, I see what looks like a trap door a few feet from me. It's not ideal, but it would probably be more secure than being out in the open the way I am.

I crawl across the open space and dig my fingers into the gap between the floor boards. The door opens easily, and I can see that there's a small room below me. I drop through the opening, pulling the door closed behind me. A moment later, I remember that there are boxes near the hidden door. Using a small push of air magic, I nudge them over the door to conceal it more. It has to be enough.

Darkness surrounds me, and I breathe a sigh of relief. I can hear muted sounds above me, so I know I'm not completely safe yet. But this space is more secure than the warehouse office I'd tried earlier. A few minutes pass, and silence descends upon me. My stomach growls, but before I can grab a granola bar, images from the apartment flash through my head. Any desire for food dissipates as I relive the worst moment of my life again. I force myself to drink some water, then settle down with my head on my pack again. Hopefully this hiding place will work for now.

The surge of adrenaline wanes, and I know that I won't escape again tonight. If I'm found, I will be caught. I don't have the energy to run anymore, and I'm not convinced I can win a fight against who- or whatever is hunting me.

BRADY

"Are you sure?" I ask Griff again, knowing I'm pissing him off.

"I just fucking told you. I'm sure. If you want to cast the spells, be my guest," he bites back at me.

As much as I deserve his annoyance, I can't help the growl that escapes me. "I want to be sure, that's all," I answer, glancing at Nico as if I expect him to take my side. I know better.

Realizing my attention has shifted to him, Nico shakes his head. "She's alone. Just like Griff said. But you can smell that, so you don't need my shadows to confirm his spell. Why don't you admit what you're really wondering?"

Leave it to Nico to see through my bullshit in record time. "Fine. I can't help wondering what's so special about this girl. We gave our word that we'd protect her, but we have no idea what we're protecting her from. All we really know is that she's holed up inside the entrance to our hideout."

"So, let's go ask her," Nico suggests. I love that he's so blunt and forward about things, but I'm not sure that's the right path with this.

"And what if she really is as dangerous as they said, and she ends up killing one of us because we spooked her?" Griff offers.

"Griff is right. We don't know what kind of powers she has, and if we just burst in, she'll get scared and may even hurt herself. Or draw those goons back," I agree.

Nico doesn't look amused by our reluctance, but after a minute, he shrugs and leans back against the wall, letting the shadows conceal him from view. Arguing with my team isn't going to make this mission any easier, so I let it go. Of course, I know Griff is right, and she's alone. I knew before Nico confirmed it. I can scent her, and hers is the only scent inside the small shack besides ours.

The aforementioned goons passed by our hidden entrance, but they didn't sense or see the girl, so they kept moving. Until we arrived and led them away from here. I wanted nothing more than to shift and attack them, but I have to keep my shifted form hidden as much as possible. I won't be able to do my job if people are searching for a snow leopard shifter in the city. It's not like my kind is common here. Really, none of us are. Not many snow leopards would be traveling with, much less living and working with, a warlock like Griffin, and a shadow wielder like Nico. But here we are.

GRIFFIN

Brady pisses me off, and he knows it. I'm sure it's all part of some stupid alpha cat bullshit he feels compelled to start. I don't care who's "in charge," as long as it's not me. I don't want that kind of responsibility.

We should be more focused on the next job, though, and less on babysitting this fledgling witch who supposedly has more power than we can imagine. I'm reluctant to believe that, although her guardians were genuinely afraid for her life. The only reason I agreed was that Nico asked me to. I'm used to Brady being a bleeding heart; trying to protect anyone weaker than we are. Nico is not usually so easily influenced by a sob story.

I know, I know. I shouldn't be out for myself when I have two of the best partners ever on my team. I should care about them and their desires as much as my own. But why should I lie about it? Money is my top priority, along with staying off the authorities' radar.

I promise, I'm not actually an asshole. It's just hard for me to let down my guard and believe people when everyone is out to scam everyone else. I'm not falling for it. The more we watch this witch, the more I believe that she does need protection. Why wouldn't they teach her how to use her powers?

I want to ask, but I know Brady and Nico don't have the answers. Asking would just be a waste of time, leading to speculation and assumption. Neither will help us keep the girl safe. And I gave my word that I would help my team do just that.

"She's sleeping. Can't we take a break and get some food or something? Maybe discuss the next job?" I ask instead, changing the subject to what needs to be our priority.

Nico's amber eyes meet my blue ones. "You can go get food and bring it back. Then we can discuss the job, while we keep an eye on her."

I glance at Brady, who seems content to let Nico take the lead on this. Fuck. I don't want to be relegated to errand boy, but it seems like that's what I'm doing. "Fine. I'll be back in a few." Storming off isn't mature, but I'm too annoyed to care. I don't bother to ask what anyone wants to eat, either.

We've been a team long enough for me to know what they'd want. I'm just enough of an asshole to not care at the moment. I'll grab sandwiches from Enzo's and if they don't like it, they can go get something else. While I'm in line to order, it occurs to me that maybe I should grab something for the girl, too. She's alone and scared, and I'm sure she's hungry.

NICO

I can't help feeling like a creep for using my shadows to watch the girl sleep. Griff storms off to get food, and I know that Brady has pissed him off again. We should be working together as a team; instead, we're arguing and debating why we decided to protect this girl.

We know nothing about her, except that she's supposed to be a super-powerful elemental witch who's been in hiding since birth. That means she probably doesn't know what she is or hasn't been taught how to use her powers. All in all, this is not an ideal situation. But instead of arguing either side, I'm keeping my thoughts to myself. Mostly.

I wasn't about to leave the girl here alone while we went to get food. And I refuse to leave her in Brady's care by himself. There's too much that could go wrong. I love my friend, but he's not great at follow-through. Besides, I gave my word along side of his, so I'm responsible for this dark-haired beauty who is currently sleeping in what's essentially our entry way.

Part of me wants to bring her the rest of the way inside, but I know there's a chance that would scare her even more than she already is. And given that we can always use one of the other entrances to the hideout, she's not really in the way.

I'd like to know what or who is hunting her. The guardians should have shared that with us at least. But they didn't. Instead, they urged us to take on this responsibility with no real understanding of what we are up against.

"I'm gonna go out and patrol until Griff gets back," Brady says, standing up and stretching before shifting into his animal form.

"I'll keep an eye on her from here," I answer, focusing my attention back to my shadows. I suspect that patrolling is an excuse to step away, as Brady has been acting strange since he first scented the girl. There's something he's not telling us, but I haven't figured out what it is yet.

Pushing my shadows closer to the sleeping figure, I try to spy without waking her. I can taste her magic through the darkness flowing from me. She may be as powerful as her guardians claimed, but she's definitely a little wild. There's a layer of darkness in her as well. I'm not sure they knew about that. Given that we received the message to start our responsibilities, I doubt we can ask them about it now. It seemed pretty clear at our last meeting that they were not expecting to survive this situation.

I hate that she's all alone in the world now. If she had any other family, we wouldn't have been approached for this. We're not exactly the warm and cuddly types. But when protection is the goal, warm and cuddly don't always factor into the equation. We're not babysitters, so it should be okay.

Even as I have the thought, something about it feels wrong. The desire I have in relation to this girl—it's not to protect her, but to own her. With the way Brady has been reacting to her, I don't want this to turn into a pissing contest. So, I intend to push these desires and feelings down, focus on the job, and see how this all plays out.

With Brady and Griff both gone, I'm forced to make sure she stays safe. So, even though I want to keep my distance right now, when she screams in terror, I can't fight the urge to bust into the room and scoop her into my arms.

"It's okay, dewdrop. I've got you." I wrap her tightly in my embrace, and she calms for a moment before jerking awake. "I won't hurt you. Just a nightmare. You're fine; I promise."

"Where, where am I? Who are you?" she asks, blinking to clear the sleep from her eyes and probably push away the images that caused her to scream.

"I'm Nico, and you are actually in my home. Sort of." Her face pales, and I rush to comfort her. "It's okay. We knew you were here, and it really saves us from having to bring you with us. This will sound a little crazy, but I promise we're not going to hurt you. Your guardians asked my friends and me to take care of you once they…" I can't finish the thought, because the moment I say guardians, tears fill her eyes.

"I'm sorry, dewdrop. It's okay to cry, but you're safe now," I assure her, still holding her tightly. "Is it okay if I carry you into the main living area? There's more room, plus I can get you some pillows and blankets to make you more comfortable."

She's barely able to respond through her sobs, but manages a quiet, "O-okay."

ZOLA

Overwhelmed does not even come close to how I'm feeling right now. The nightmare that wakes me is an even more violent version of events, that crested with me being gutted by some dark figure who had just killed my guardians.

Waking up in a strange man's arms should have sent me over the edge. I should have started swinging the moment my eyes met his. But there's something about this man, this sorcerer...no, that's not right. He's not exactly a sorcerer. My magic senses his, but it's different—muted somehow.

I can't explain why, but I feel safe with him, with Nico. Even before he mentions my guardians asking him and his friends to protect me, I know he won't hurt me. I should be wondering about my sanity. Being hunted by some unknown force, and still trusting the first man I meet? Probably not the best idea. My magic doesn't sense danger, though, so I'm giving him a chance.

I doubt he knows the extent of my powers when I still don't, anyway. He carries me through a door I hadn't seen when I entered this room.

PROTECTORS

ZOLA

Nico settles me onto a couch in front of a fireplace. I sink in a bit, reveling in the softness and velvety feel of the fabric against my hands. Before I can ask how they can have a fire underground, Nico places a fluffed pillow behind me, and wraps me in the most luxurious blanket I've ever felt.

"Are you hungry? Griff went to get food. I can ask him to grab you something," Nico offers.

"I'm starved, and so thirsty," I admit, cheeks flushing. I guess I'm thirsty in more ways than one, I realize as my eyes survey the man standing over me.

"Any food allergies, dislikes, favorites I should note?" he asks, completely focused on me. It's a little unnerving how he doesn't break eye contact.

"Um, anything is fine. Turkey bacon ranch with spinach and tomato is my favorite wrap. But honestly, I'll eat whatever. I'm not trying to be difficult," I insist.

Nico chuckles and shakes his head while typing something on his phone as he grabs me a bottle of water from the fridge. As I sip, I hear something and bristle, even though his demeanor doesn't change.

A tall, broad, strawberry-blond man walks into the room as if he belongs here. Something about him feels familiar, but dangerous. He stares at me as if he's a predator and I'm his prey. It's more unnerving than Nico's penchant for eye contact.

"Nico, what the fuck do you think you're doing? We agreed to watch, not to interfere unless she was being attacked. Did something happen while I was gone?" the man growls.

Nico shakes his head. "Brady, it's okay. She had a nightmare, and I was worried she'd hurt herself. So, I woke her and brought her in here. It's fine. I've texted Griff to grab her a wrap from Enzo's. She's safer in here with us than out there where she can be found easily."

The beast of a man, Brady, is clearly torn between Nico's explanation and his shock at finding me inside his home. I tense, suddenly afraid that he's going to turn me away. Surely not, though, since Nico said they'd promised to protect me. Right?

No sense in cowering in the face of danger, I tell myself. "You don't have to speak about me as if I'm not sitting right here. If I'm in your way, I'll leave, though I have nowhere safe to go. You don't have to worry about whatever promises you made to Raj or Amara. I absolve you of your responsibilities. I can take care of myself."

As I speak, I force myself to stand and move toward the door. Brady stares at me, not moving, except a muscle in his jaw. I make it three steps before Nico stops me. "Dewdrop, you don't have to leave. Brady is just mad that he wasn't the one to make that call. For some reason, he thinks he's the boss around here," he says, as dark shadows wrap around us, cradling me to his chest.

Nico turns his head toward Brady. "Isn't that right, Brady? We don't want her to leave, do we?" The forceful note in Nico's voice makes the other man shudder. I wonder if he's afraid of the shadows that are currently wrapped around me like a blanket, comforting, soft, and much warmer than I would have expected.

"He's right. It's not safe for you out there. I just wasn't ready to bring you in here. As Nico reminded me, it doesn't matter what my plans were. Your safety and comfort come first. Please don't leave because of me," Brady insists. Something flashes in his eyes, and for a moment, I sense more than danger in him.

Before I can respond, another man storms into the room. Slightly shorter than Brady, muscular, but not in a gym bro way, with sandy blond hair, he stops short when he sees me. His face contorts, and a spark of magic lights up his fingers. My own magic responds, but I tamp it down before it can reach out. What does that mean?

The newcomer takes a step toward me, and I duck behind Nico before I realize that I'm actually terrified of what just happened between us. My magic has never done that before, and I have no idea what it could mean. Instinctively I know that Nico is safe, and my hands grip his waist from behind. His hand lands on mine, his shadows reaching out to caress my cheek.

"It's okay, dewdrop. Griff won't hurt you. He may be the most awkward of us, which is saying something. Especially with how you were just introduced to Brady. You have my word; no one here will hurt you. I won't allow it," Nico says quietly. There's a conviction in his voice that reassures me about my unconscious decision to trust him.

He turns his attention back to his friends, and I watch as the two men seem to defer to him. I don't get the impression that he's their leader, but they definitely respect him. "Give her some space. Stop growling at her. We still need to discuss the job, and we will, once she's settled in."

Brady nods, takes a bag from Griff, and heads to the table. Griff shakes his head and takes the other bags to the table. Neither man makes an effort to talk to me again as Nico grabs food and leads me back to the couch. "I promise they're not always assholes. This situation is a bit out of our usual comfort zone, so it's going to take some time to adjust to. I meant it when I said I won't let anyone hurt you. I just need you to trust me, and do what I ask. Okay?"

His dark eyes lock with mine, and I nod. "I trust you, Nico. Thank you."

GRIFFIN

As soon as my magic sparks at her, I know what that means, and it terrifies me. No matter how I felt about this job before, I know that I will give my life to protect her. This girl, this witch, is my elskede—my beloved—my fated mate. I grew up hearing stories of this connection, but I've always thought that's just what they were...stories. Clearly, my coven knew what they were talking about.

I'm not sure if I'm relieved or concerned that she seems to have no idea what that reaction means. I know I'll have to explain it to her at some point. It's too soon. I need to give her time to get used to us and this situation.

I don't know how to act without making this weirder than I already have. So, I sit at the table with Brady and start eating while Nico gets my elskede settled in. I can't help noticing how easy they are in each other's presence, which leads me to wonder if he's bonded with her too. It's not completely unheard of, but would be a challenge for us.

Staring at her won't make anyone more comfortable, so I settle for stealing glances as I eat. I try to keep my focus on Brady and discussing the next job. We can't talk too loudly, because it's never a good idea to share our work with outsiders, even if she's my mate.

"We can't put it off any longer. The job has to be done tonight, girl or no girl. We can leave her here, so she's out of the way and safe. Or one of us can stay with her. It doesn't matter how we do it, the job needs to be completed," Brady says quietly.

If my elskede overheard this conversation, she would have no idea that the job involves murder. Okay, technically, assassination, but still. Killing is killing, and I'm sure this innocent girl would have no part in that.

"Agreed. But if someone stays with her, it should be Nico. She seems more comfortable with him," I offer.

"I understand that, but we need him for the plan to work. It's better if we can secure her here alone, and go get it done ourselves," Brady insists.

Nico pulls out the chair between us and sits down. "Perhaps Griff can cast a protection spell, or a lock on the hideout to keep her here and prevent anyone else from coming inside? Then the three of us are free to complete the job without being concerned for Dewdrop's safety."

The endearment is all I need to know that my suspicions are correct. Nico's magic must have had the same reaction to her that mine did. I don't mind the idea of sharing my beloved with my friend. We're more like brothers anyway, and it's not like we've never experimented with each other. Brady has always been less comfortable with his sexuality, so part of me hopes that he's not bonded with her too. Although, if he was, it would definitely make things easier as far as us keeping her safe. I push the thought away, knowing that there will be time to consider that and figure out what we need to do later.

"I can cast a protection spell on her, and a lockdown spell on the hideout. I won't be able to make it so the three of us have access, but as long as I'm with you, and you're not acting against me, you'll be able to come in with me," I explain. The intricacies of the spell aren't important, so I don't bother explaining them.

BRADY

I'm not sure what is going on with my friends, but it's clear that they're already attached to this girl who is supposed to be a job for us. Much like the assassination we're supposed to complete tonight. The mayor is involved with some unsavory characters who are attempting to enact some legislature that would restrict the rights of anyone in the supernatural community. Of course, we're against that idea, so the guild sent us this assignment. From the research we've done, the mayor isn't an issue; he's just an idiot who's being used by those who wish us harm.

As much as I want to focus on taking out the man named Jericho, who is our target, I can't help finding myself distracted by the subtle scent of four elements mixed together wafting toward me. My shifter growls, and the hair on the back of my neck stands up. Fuck. This complicates things. I can't afford a mate bond right now, especially when it seems as if she may be bonded to my friends too.

I push the thought away. I have no desire for a mate, and won't be accepting a bond with anyone. Feelings get in the way of the job. They make you weak and vulnerable. I am neither of those things. I refuse to let a woman tear down what I've fought so hard for.

Focus on the job. That's all. Push the feelings down. With that repeating in my head, I turn my attention back to my team.

"What do you need for your spells? And how long will they take? We have a few hours to prepare, but this has to be done tonight. The fundraiser is being hosted by the museum, and everyone will be there at seven. We're only going to have a small window to catch Jericho alone," I explain, knowing that we don't need the reminder.

Nico nods, looking to Griff for details. "I have everything I need already for both spells. It'll take me about half an hour to cast the protection, and half that for the lock. It's probably a good idea to let her know what we're doing, though, so she doesn't fight us or try to follow."

"Griff, we can't tell her about the job," I insist.

"I'm not saying that, B. I think we should tell her I need to cast a protection spell on her, and a lockdown spell on the hideout. That's all. We just tell her we have to go out for a bit, and want to keep her safe. Nico can explain it," Griff answers.

I can't help wondering why he wants Nico to be the only one in direct contact with the girl, but maybe it makes casting the spells easier. I can't stress over that right now. I have to figure out how we're going to pull off this job with half the city in the area.

NICO

Since I've been volunteered to explain things to Dewdrop without actually telling her about our job, I ponder what I'll say while I eat. Listening to Brady and Griff's back and forth has questions running through my mind. Griff's reaction to her is enough to assume that he's having the same feelings of attachment as I am. Add to that the way Brady can barely take his eyes off her, and they keep flashing amber as if he's struggling to keep his shift back, and I'm pretty sure we might have an issue here.

If all three of us are fated to this witch, it's a wonderful and awful thing. Sharing won't be an issue for us, but control will. I hope that once she's more comfortable with us, that my dewdrop will take the reins of this and force the guys in line. Otherwise, there's gonna be some infighting, and it's gonna get uncomfortable.

Brady's right, though. We need to focus on Jericho. And to do that, we have to make sure Dewdrop is safe. We can't put ourselves in harm's way tonight if we're distracted by her. And mate bonds are enough of a distraction. Perhaps we should discuss it after the job tonight.

I shake my head to push the thought away as I drop onto the couch next to her. "Sorry for the shop talk. We have some stuff that has to be taken care of tonight, though."

Zola looks at me. "Do I have to stay here? Or can I go with you?" The complete trust in her eyes floors me. She has no reason to believe that we're going to keep her safe, but here we are.

"I need you to stay here. It'll be safer for you, and we'll be able to get things done quicker. But Griff needs to cast a couple of spells to make sure you're protected while we're gone. Is that okay?" I ask, wondering if she'll agree or ask questions.

"I might be okay with that. Am I allowed to ask what spells? I understand that your business is your own, and I'm not asking about that. But I don't feel comfortable letting someone cast on me without knowing the spell and the reason. Please," she says. Tears glisten in her eyes, and I understand that if I push her without explaining, she will agree, but it will hurt her.

"One spell is a protection. It will keep anyone from getting close to you or harming you while we're gone. The other will be on the hideout itself, to prevent anyone from entering besides us. What that means, though, is that you'll need to promise to stay here, and not try to get away. The second spell essentially locks you in and everyone else out," I explain.

"So, I'll be a prisoner for a while," she responds, a tear sliding down her cheek.

"Oh, dewdrop," I wipe the tear from her cheek and cup her face in my hands. "I understand it feels that way, and you're not wrong. But it's only to keep you safe, and only while the three of us need to be away. Can you trust me enough for that?"

I barely stop myself from holding my breath while she considers what I've asked her. A strange thought crosses my mind, and I suddenly understand how characters in books can hold their breath without realizing it.

Her chocolate eyes meet mine, and she nods. "You promised to keep me safe, and I trust you. If you say that he needs to cast these spells and I need to stay here for that to happen, I'm okay with that. I don't like being a prisoner, but I'll deal with it for a little while."

A grin spreads across my face and I pull her into my arms. "You can stay in my room while we're gone. It's definitely the cleanest. I have books or you can watch TV. There's a soundproof spell on the room so no one will even know you're in there. Not that they'd be able to get inside anyway," I say.

She smiles back at me, and a weight lifts from my chest. "Where's my bag?" she asks, as if just realizing that she had things with her when she escaped being hunted. I glance around, realizing that I left it in the outer room.

"I'll get it for you," I offer, standing. When Brady gestures at me, I sit back down. "Or Brady will. I'm sorry I missed it when you were having your nightmare."

"It's okay. I don't even remember what I tossed into it. I was in such a hurry to get out of there. Do you know what's hunting me?"

The question catches me off guard. I would have expected her to know exactly what danger she's in, but from her expression and tone, she has no idea. "Your guardians didn't tell you?"

Zola shakes her head. Before I can answer, Brady is standing next to us, holding out her bag. "It doesn't look like anyone has messed with it, but please check it while we're still here. I'd rather not get surprised while we're out."

She looks at him for a long moment, then nods and drags the bag open, dumping the contents onto the coffee table in front of us.

Fear of Abandonment

ZOLA

I HAVE NO IDEA why I trust Nico already. Besides the fact that he didn't kill me when he found me, and he actually took care of me, I don't know this man. I should run away; not agree to stay here while they do whatever. For all I know, the three of them have dates and I'll be sitting here waiting for them to return while they're off fucking some bitches.

Okay, that thought might have been a little harsh. And if I'm honest with myself, the thought of them fucking other women makes me unreasonably angry. Makes sense with Nico, I guess, since I thought he liked me. Not so much with Griff or Brady. Neither of them has really been flirty or even kind to me. Besides the not killing me part. Who knows? Maybe they're going to meet with the people who want me and they'll sell me for a profit.

All I really know is that I don't want them to leave me here, protection spells or not. I agree to stay here, but can't stop trying to come up with a reason to go with them. When Brady orders me to dump my bag out for them to search through, I stare at him for a minute. I'm not thrilled about anyone going through my underwear, but that's not my biggest hesitation. I really don't remember what I threw in the bag. I was thinking about protection and running; staying hidden. Oh, well. It's not like I could stop them from searching my things anyway.

I dump the bag out on the table in front of me. Dropping the empty bag on the floor, I grab my notebook and hold it to my chest tightly. "This is personal," I say, clutching it tightly. I don't want to admit that this is where I keep my research on targets. The last thing I need is for these guys to realize that I kill people in my free time.

"I don't want to violate your privacy, but I need you to let Griff check that out. He'll be able to sense if there's any magic on it that isn't yours," Brady insists, motioning to the book. "Don't worry, he won't read it."

Griff steps closer. "I just need to touch it; you don't even have to let go." He reaches out and I fight my racing heart to place the book into his opened hand. My fingers brush against his palm, and a spark of electricity jolts me. I jerk my hand back quickly, leaving my damning evidence in his hand. All he has to do is open the notebook and they'll know. Then will they turn me in? Or worse?

Part of me wants to grab the book and run, but Nico's arms wrap around me from behind, and tingles dart up my arms. It's similar to what just happened with Griff, but less jarring. What the fuck is going on here? I don't have time to dissect my body's or my magic's reaction to these men. Not with Brady staring at the notebook like it holds the secrets of the universe and he's dying to know everything.

A moment later, Griff holds the unopened notebook out to me. Nico relaxes his grip so I can snatch it without touching the warlock. "I won't violate your privacy, elskede. No magic has touched that book besides yours until mine just did. It's safe."

"Thank you. It's just, um, personal. I don't care about the rest of my things; touch whatever. But this is just for me," I stammer, wondering if my explanation will make them want to read it more than they already do.

Nico and Brady exchange a look when Griff gives my book back, and I wonder if that's about my book or the foreign word he refers to me with. I need to remember to ask what that means, but I don't think now is the right moment.

The three men spend a few minutes looking through the contents of my bag. I wasn't kidding when I said I didn't care if they touched things, but I can't stand here and watch. I turn away slightly and open my book. A strong desire to check for myself and make sure no one has messed with it comes over me. Flipping through the pages, I nearly forget that I'm not alone, letting myself get caught up in my research.

BRADY

My partners bonding with my fated mate was not on my bingo card for this year, but here we are. With the endearments they've both used while talking to her, and the way Griff's magic has sparked twice, I'm sure that's what's happening here. Fuck.

I want nothing more than to ignore her scent and the way it calls to me. I know she's dusha moya, my soul, but that doesn't mean I'm ready for it. And I'm not sure how I feel about the idea that I'll have to share her. Polyamory isn't unusual, but it is a little bit out of my comfort zone. I guess I should be thankful that she's not bonded to strangers or, worse, my enemies. At least with my brothers, I can work through my feelings without worrying that someone is taking her from me.

The three of us need to discuss this without her in the way. How we move forward depends on the guys and how they react to knowing we're all bonded to the same witch. I can tell that she's more comfortable with Nico than me or Griff, and as much as that grates at me, it's for the best. Nico is the least social of us; he's also the most patient.

I shake those thoughts away, uncomfortable with how quickly my subconscious went from refusing to acknowledge the bond to claiming her as ours. Push it down. Put it away. Focus on the job. Jericho has to die. Tonight.

"We need to get ready." It's not like I need to announce it, but I can't let us get distracted. Zola jumps at my words, and guilt spears through me for startling dusha moya. Fuck. I have to stop thinking of her that way. She's a complication, that's all.

Since we didn't find anything suspicious in her bag, Nico helps her pack everything back inside. A pang of jealousy races through me at how easily he touches her and the way she leans into it. That should be me.

Fuck. No, Brady. Let it go. Push it down. I do not want a mate bond. Maybe if I tell myself that enough, I'll start to believe it. I scoff at the idea.

"What's up?" Griff asks.

"It's nothing," I answer, pushing past him to grab my gear from my room. "We just have to focus on the job."

GRIFFIN

Something is up with Brady, but I'm not sure if it has to do with the job or the girl. Maybe my earlier thoughts were right, and he's fighting the pull of his mating bond with her. That would explain why he won't get near her, or even try to touch her. His clear discomfort has to be obvious to her as well.

Now is not the time to have a conversation about fated mates and bonds, though. Brady is right about one thing—we have to focus on the job. And since we have to also protect the girl, my first priority is to cast the protection spell on her and the lockdown spell on the hideout.

I duck into my room to gather the supplies I need for each spell. I can cast the lockdown spell first, since it's faster, and I don't need anyone for that. I grab a candle, bay leaf, strip of oak bark, and a clove. Taking the ingredients to my altar, I light the candle and grab a bloodstone. I crush the bay, oak, and clove together with my mortar and pestle, adding a few drops of the wax from the candle. I coat the bloodstone with the mixture and focus my intent on making a shield around the hideout that only allows Brady, Nico, or myself to pass through.

After a few minutes of concentration, I feel the magic spread through the air, fusing with the walls, ceiling, and floor. It would have been easier to just protect one room, but I'm sure Nico doesn't want Zola to feel trapped any more than she already does.

With the hideout spell in place, I turn my attention to a protection spell for Zola. To do that, I need to clean the mortar and pestle, then search for a piece of rowan wood. Once I have those, I grab a pinch of rosemary and black salt, add a few drops of cedar essential oil, and grind the mixture together, burning a bit of the rowan wood to add its ashes to the mix.

When it's the texture I want, I roll a smoky quartz in it, then carve a sigil in the side of the stone. While the mixture soaks into the stone, I focus on creating a silver bracelet to contain the stone. It's easier to use my magic for this than to forge the bracelet by hand. As much as I would enjoy taking the time to create this particular piece with my bare hands, there isn't time. I work the strands of silver into intricate knots with the intent to keep her safe, and prevent anyone from harming her.

The moment I have the silver completed; I add the stone to an open scrollwork cage in the center of the bracelet. Perfect.

I glance at the clock and realize that I've completed both spells in less time than I'd expected. There's still one more part to the personal protection spell, but I need the girl for that. I hope that she accepts the bracelet without any objections. The spell works better if there's no resistance.

Carrying the bracelet, I leave my room, wondering how to approach this, and if I should just tell her that she's my fated. Our eyes meet, and I realize that she's not ready for that yet. That can wait.

"This is for the protection spell. I need you to wear it. But once you put it on, you can't take it off, or the spell will break," I explain, holding up the bracelet.

"It's beautiful. Did you make this?" she asks breathily.

I nod, and she offers her left wrist, then hesitates. "Does it matter which arm?"

"Left is perfect, elskede," I answer, clipping the silver around her arm. She shivers as the magic works its way around her.

"That felt weird. Did it work?" her eyes are wide as she asks me. I hold up a hand to scan her, and can sense that the magic is wrapped around her tightly.

"It did. You should be safe now," I reply.

Worry melts from her expression and she throws her arms around me, hugging tightly. "Thank you." My arms wrap around her without thinking. She holds me as if I'm her salvation, and I breathe her in. Part of me wants to admit what my soul knows; that we're meant to be, but now is not the time.

Instead, I hug her back, then ease myself away before the hard on in my pants gives me away. "You're welcome. We will keep you safe. You can trust us," I promise. And at that moment, I know that I will do anything to keep her safe. The personal cost won't matter. I will lay down my life for this woman, if it means keeping her safe.

Did Amara and Raj know when they tasked us with protecting their ward? How could they? It can't be a coincidence though, that the three men trusted with protecting this uber powerful witch just happen to be her fated mates. Can it?

NICO

As much as I don't want to leave Zola here while we take care of Jericho, I know there is no other option. If we don't complete our contract, the guild will take us out and find someone who will. And it's not like we're opposed to killing him. He's an asshole. I can't explain the amount of pleasure it will bring me to drain the life from him.

Surely, the guild would understand the current situation. Our fated mate arrived and needs protection. No one could fault us for wanting to keep her safe instead of fulfilling our contract. Of course, that thought hinges on being able to contact Brynn and ask for an extension of sorts. Which I know is nearly impossible.

Okay, so an extension is out. We just need to get the job done as quickly as we can so that Dewdrop isn't left alone for very long. We can handle that. Get in, take Jericho out, come home. Easy peasy. Yes, I know how cheesy that sounds.

Once we have our gear gathered, the guys and I meet in the kitchen. "The spells worked, so she'll be fine," Griff assures us. I can tell that he and I are on the same page with protecting our girl, even if we haven't discussed the fact that we're both mated to her.

"We won't be gone long," I say to Zola when she wanders in.

"Why can't I go with you? I'll be safe with the protection spell." The fear in her eyes nearly makes me cave. But Brady steps between us.

"No. You have to stay here. We'll be back as soon as we can. There's plenty of snacks and drinks. Take a shower if you want, or a bath. Watch some TV, read a book. Take a nap. You'll be fine," he insists. A muscle in his jaw twitches when she pouts at him.

I pull her into my arms, and she relaxes into my embrace. "Trust me, I don't want to leave you here any more than you want to stay without us. But knowing that you'll be safe is more important right now. We have to go, but we will be back."

She looks up at me, tears in her eyes. "Okay." Before I can stop myself, I lean down and press my lips to her forehead. Her cheeks flush and she backs away from me. I won't apologize, because I'm not sorry, and it didn't hurt her.

"Remember, stay here, and you'll stay safe," I say as I walk away.

Griff calls over his shoulder, "Please don't try to leave. It'll set off the spell, and I don't want to hurt you."

She nods and waves as the door closes behind us. The sooner we get this job done, the better.

ZOLA

For a moment, I'm shocked that Griff warns me about the spell on their home. I hadn't considered that it would keep me in as much as it would keep other people out. That's not a bad thing, though, so I don't balk at it.

After they leave, I find myself snooping around a little. I have no idea if they use protection spells on their rooms or belongings, so I don't go too crazy with it. Sticking to the community spaces seems the safest. I look through the books on the shelf, then peruse the movies on the next shelf over.

Within ten minutes, I'm bored to tears. I collapse on the couch, pulling the blanket Nico gave me earlier around me. These men are definitely easy on the eyes. I think about each of them, letting my mind wander.

They're all attractive, and seem to be interested in me. Except Brady. He's hot, but doesn't seem to like me at all. I can't quite put my finger on what it is about him, but I can't deny that I'm interested in him. It sucks that we're not on the same page.

I spend a little time lamenting that I didn't figure out what they were doing, then decide to let it go. I have my own secrets to worry about. I pull my notebook out of my bag and flip back to the last section. With John taken care of, I've completed all the missions I set for myself. I officially have nothing to do now. Other than being in hiding and starting my life over without my guardians, things look pretty good.

I'm proud of myself for looking at the bright side, even if it's ridiculous. My family is dead, I'm homeless, and I can't go back to school. How is this situation good? I barely stifle a laugh at the idea. I doze on the couch for a while, letting myself relax in this safe space.

A noise pulls me from sleep. What the fuck? Someone is pounding on the hidden door of the hideout. No one is supposed to know about that door. Right? The noise gets louder, and I decide that hiding is a better idea than sitting here. I grab the blanket and my bag, race to Nico's room and lock the door. I crawl into the bottom of his closet and curl into the smallest ball I can. Tears stream down my face and I try to breathe while panic takes over.

The people hunting me must have found me, and I never even learned what they wanted me for. All I know is that my guardians were scared I'd be killed. Apparently, my parents were concerned about the same thing before their deaths. Come to think of it, that does not bode well for my safety.

Terror grips me, and I fight to stay silent. I can't tell if the pounding is still happening, or if they've broken through Griff's spell already and are inside. Griff and Nico are gonna be so upset that someone actually broke in, and maybe that I'm dead. I grip my bracelet and beg the gods to spare me.

CRY FOR HELP

BRADY

"WOULD YOU TWO STOP pining over the girl and focus?" I growl as we pull up to the museum. It looks like guests are utilizing the valet, but I'll be leaving our car on the street for easy access. We can't exactly murder a man, then wait at the valet stand while they pull the car around. The thought almost makes me chuckle. Almost.

"We're not pining over the girl," Griff insists. "I can't help being concerned about her. She was terrified that we were leaving her alone."

"Exactly," Nico agrees. "And with what she's just been through, you can't expect her to be okay by herself. We know the job has to get done, but keeping her safe is important too."

It's not that I disagree with either of them, I just need them to forget her for a little while and help me with this job. "I understand that you're worried about her. All I'm asking is for you to shift focus to the job for a while. The sooner we get this done, the quicker we get back home and make sure she's okay."

I step out of the car, adjust my suit jacket, and head toward the front door. Without waiting for the guys to follow, I pull the invitation from my pocket and hand it to the security guard at the door. He barely glances at it and ushers me through. I can't help wondering what the point of the invitations is if they can be forged so easily. But that's Brynn's thing, and it's not like I can ask them about it right now.

Once inside the museum, I scan the room for our target, as if I'm looking for my date or a friend. A few people nod as if greeting me, and I respond in kind, pretending that they might actually know me. The only thing they know is that I look like a guy with money. We both know that's what they're responding to.

Women in opulent dresses look me up and down as I pass by them. If I were in the market for company tonight, I have no doubt one of them would be a willing participant. But I'm not. I'm here for the job. My part is to get eyes on the target, then report his location to Griff and Nico. Once I find Jericho,

Griff will enter the gala and get in position. When he's in place, Nico will come in. Then the fun will start.

"I've got eyes," I say. "Southwest corner of the ball room, near the bar."

GRIFFIN

As much as I hate to admit it, Brady may be right. It's possible that Nico and I are too worried about Zola to focus. I realize this when I almost miss his direction when he spots the target. *Fuck, Griff, get your head in the game.*

"Invitation?" the guard asks, and I feel his annoyance in the single word. Everyone knows to present them at the entrance. I just got distracted and didn't have it out.

"Oh, sorry. Excited to meet up with my girl," I grin, hoping that the guard takes me for a lovesick fool. The man rolls his eyes at me and gestures for me to go through. Okay, time to blend in and find my vantage point.

I follow the crowd into the ballroom, eyeing the southwest corner of the room while heading in the opposite direction. Zeroing in on our target is easy. Jericho is a slimy looking thug with slicked back black hair and a clean-shaven face. He looks like one of those mafia guys in the movies, and it makes me want to laugh. How is this guy dangerous enough to make it onto our radar?

"Is it just me, or does this guy look like a joke?" I ask, careful to keep my voice low enough that only the mic picks it up.

"You're not wrong," Brady responds. "Are you in position yet?"

"Sorry, got held up at the door. I'm almost there," I answer. It doesn't matter that we've had comms on the whole time and he probably knows that my issue at the door was my own doing. Since he isn't calling me out on it, I'm not pointing it out.

I slip through the crowd easily and find the door that leads to the back of house and around to the bar. The door clicks closed behind me, and I signal Nico. "I'm in."

Not waiting for his response, I continue to follow the hall around to my final destination. My job is to wait in the bar storage room for Nico's signal, then have the portal ready for us to get out of here. With a little luck, we'll be finished here and back home in an hour or so.

NICO

At Griff's signal, I head inside. I'm the interceptor tonight, so I have to actually talk to this asshole. I hate having drawn the short straw for this, even as much as I'm going to enjoy watching his life drain from him.

I grab a glass of champagne from a tray as a server passes by. We have to keep up appearances, right? Might as well have a drink, then. I down the contents of the glass before setting it down on the next server's tray.

My eyes are locked on the target as I weave through the crowd. As I approach him, a pain shoots through my heart and I hear Griff gasp in my ear. I freeze, stopping short of making contact with Jericho. "What the hell was that?" I ask, looking around to see if Griff is visible.

"I don't know, but I felt it, too. Brady?" Griff asks.

It takes a minute for him to answer, but Brady sounds annoyed. "What are you two talking about? Let's get this job done."

I shake the feeling off and move forward again, playing it off to those around me as if I've just had too much to drink and needed a moment. Keeping Jericho in my sights, I move around him to lean against the wall for a moment. I can't explain why, but my chest hurts and I'm struggling to breathe.

"Nico, what are you doing? We need to focus," Brady says in my ear.

Before I can answer, Griff breaks in, "We need to get back to the hideout now. She's in danger. Someone got through the lockdown spell."

Fuck. I knew we shouldn't have left her alone. If anything has happened to her, I will never forgive myself. And I know that Griff feels the same. "We need to finish the job first," Brady growls.

"Then you do it. Griff and I are heading back to make sure she's safe," I respond, heading toward the bar and barging through the door to the back. I don't stop until I'm standing in the storage room with Griff. "Portal?" I ask and he nods before moving his hands and creating an opening that leads us directly back to the hideout.

"You know he's gonna be pissed, right?" Griff says as the portal closes behind us.

ZOLA

I can't die like this. I won't. Amara and Raj gave their lives to protect me; I have to fight to survive. After a couple of deep breaths, I crack the closet door open and peek out into the room. I don't hear the pounding anymore, but something else catches my attention.

As much as I know I shouldn't use my powers, they are the only chance I have to survive this. I close my eyes, focusing on the air and moisture in the room. Someone is here. They got inside. With another deep breath, I shove the door open and step out.

Nico's room is empty, but I still hear footsteps and rustling. Whoever broke in is looking for something. Or for me. Either way, I'm not gonna hide in here like a coward. I may not know much about fighting, but I do know how to kill someone.

Allowing those dark desires to wash over me, I flip the lock on the bedroom door and freeze with my ear pressed to the wood. The rustling sounds further away, as if a few rooms away. I creep down the hall, heading toward the noise, making sure to muffle my steps by manipulating the air waves around me.

When I get to the open living area, I duck behind the kitchen island. There are three figures tearing the book case apart. Maybe they're not here for me after all. But what could they want? I peer around the edge of the island and focus my power, pulling the air from the closest person's body. They start choking and gasping for breath that doesn't come. The other two stop what they're doing and rush to their fallen ally.

I still can't see them well enough to tell if they are men, women, or even some sort of beasts. It doesn't matter, since it looks like they're vulnerable like my other targets. "Dave!" one shouts, and I realize it's a woman. Okay, so I've taken Dave out, and a woman is part of his crew.

Feigning bravery I definitely don't feel, I stand from my hiding spot. "What are you doing here?" My voice booms with the help of my power. The woman is leaning over Dave, and the third person moves toward me.

"Dammit, Siri, I thought you said the place was empty," the man growls. As he steps closer, I get a better look at him.

While he's humanoid, he's definitely something else, almost lizard-like in appearance.

"Stop," I order, and for a moment, he freezes. "What do you want?"

"I don't see how that's any of your business, sweet cheeks," the lizard man says with a smirk. "Unless you're offering yourself up, that is."

Eww. So not happening. "Nah, I'm good. You need to leave. Take your friends with you," I say, keeping my hands fisted at my sides so he can't see how badly I'm shaking. My heart races, and for a second, I worry that I've made a bad decision here.

"I'm not going anywhere, unless I take you with me," he counters, reaching toward me.

His hand meets a solid wall of ice, and I wonder what that means about my fight, flight, or freeze response that this is the second time this week ice has appeared to save my life. I don't have time to worry about that, because Siri steps up behind me. I can't believe I didn't see her leaving Dave. Maybe he's already dead.

"Now you've had it, bitch," she says sweetly in my ear as she grabs my arms, holding them to my sides. "Gerald, get over here and take care of this."

I try jerking out of her grasp, but it's no use. She has some sort of super strength, and I can't break her hold. Her distraction is enough for me to lose focus on the ice wall, though, and Gerald has no problem punching through it. He stalks toward me, a wide smile on his face, and I see his incisors elongating. Fuck, I'd thought he was some sort of lizard man, but it looks like he's actually part snake. This isn't looking good for me.

I push my power at him, pulling the water from him. Fear slows my progress, and just when I think he's slowing down, Gerald stops and shakes off the dry husk of skin that is peeling from his body. I stifle a gag at how disgusting it is. If I can't stop him that way, maybe I can get Siri to let go of me.

I don't have time to think with the way her arms are wrapped around me now, crushing me. Ice didn't stop them, maybe fire is the way to go. Flames lick up my arms, spreading across my torso. Closing my eyes to focus, I smell her flesh burning before she finally releases me with a scream of agony. "You shouldn't grab people like that. Especially if you don't know anything about them," I say, thrusting a burning fist into her face. "And it's not nice to call people bitches, either."

I punch her again, this time making sure to push my blaze onto her, and shove Siri into the wall. Screams fill the air as flames consume her. Turning my attention to Gerald, I see Nico and Griff step through a portal behind the lizard man. Before I can even consider attacking, shadows wrap around the intruder, and Gerald falls to the floor with his neck bent at an odd angle.

"I thought you guys had a job," I say, my eyes wide at the mess I've made by killing two people in their home.

"Are you okay, Elskede?" Griff asks, rushing to my side and patting at the flames I haven't let go yet.

"I'm fine, sorry. That's my power. See, it doesn't hurt me," I say, dropping the flames and showing him my arms.

He relaxes at the sight of my unblemished skin. Then the strangest, most wonderful thing happens. Griff pulls me into his arms and hugs me tightly. It catches me off guard and I wrap my arms around him, holding on as if my life depends on it. When he finally pushes me away, our eyes lock, and I bite my bottom lip. Griff leans closer until our lips are almost touching. I can feel his breath on my face as my eyes flutter closed.

A moment later, I'm standing there, shivering at the rush of cold air as he's jerked away from me. My eyes fly open, and I'm staring at Brady. He looks almost feral, chest heaving, face red, as he pins Griff to the wall.

"You fucking left me to finish the job alone," he growls, his arm across Griff's throat.

"Brady, let him go," Nico says, pulling his friend's arm. Brady doesn't budge, and I wonder again what job they were supposed to do.

"I'm sorry. They must have sensed that I was in trouble. These people broke in somehow, and they were trashing the place. I fought back, but if the guys hadn't got here when they did, I might not have survived," I offer, putting a hand on Brady's arm.

He releases Griff, who slides down the wall, choking for breath. I pull him away from his friend, and for some reason he follows me. "Please don't be mad at them. I don't know how they knew I needed help, other than Griff's spell being broken."

Brady stares at me for a moment. "Were you hurt?"

I shake my head, "Not really."

"Good. I have to go finish this job," he snarls. "Nico, you're with me. Griff can stay here and babysit."

Nico and Griff stare at their friend before nodding. Brady storms off, and Nico gives me an apologetic smile as he walks over to me. "I'm glad you're okay, Dewdrop. Don't worry about him. I'll calm him down." He presses a kiss to my forehead and follows Brady outside.

I help Griff up from the floor. "Thanks," he says, pulling me in for another hug.

"I'm sorry I got you in trouble," I offer.

"Nah, don't worry about it. Let's just get this cleaned up before they get back, so he doesn't have anything to bitch about besides the job," Griff says, gesturing to the bodies scattered around the room. Fuck, I nearly forgot about those.

"How are we gonna do that?" I ask, unsure of the best way to dispose of a body. I've always killed people in dark alleys and left them there. I never worried about disposal before. It's a new experience for me.

"Like this," he says, waving his hands in the air in a strange pattern. First, Dave's body turns to dust, then disappears. Then Siri's does the same, crumbling and vanishing before the pile even settles. With those two gone, Gerald is all that's left. Griff waves his hands again and the room is empty of intruders.

"That was a neat trick," I say before realizing that my reactions are probably not what he expects.

Sure enough, he's eyeing me suspiciously. "Why do I get the feeling this wasn't the first time you've killed someone?"

I stare into his eyes for a moment, debating if I should tell him the truth or not. What can it hurt now? My vigilante days are over with my guardians gone. My life here in the city is over too. So, it shouldn't matter that I've killed before.

"Probably because it's not. I'm not like a serial killer or anything," I say, pausing when I realize that I actually am. "I mean, I kinda am, but not exactly. It's a long story."

I expect Griff to shirk away from me, or judge me for my admission. Instead, he steps closer again, cupping my face in his hands. "If you want to tell your story, I would love to hear it. But no one here will ever judge you for killing someone." It seems like a weird thing to say, and my face must express that.

He laughs and lets me go. "I can't really go into details, because it could put you in danger, but the guys and I know a little bit about killing when it's needed."

"So, you're like mercenaries?" I ask, wondering if he'll actually tell me what they went to do tonight.

"I can neither confirm nor deny," he says, making a zipping motion across his lips. Well, fuck. The look on his face makes me think I'm right, but I don't want to push him for details. Especially if he meant it when he said it could put me in danger.

Confessions

ZOLA

As MUCH AS I don't want to share my secrets, I can't figure a way around it. After all, I just killed two people during a home invasion. There's no way these men will believe that was dumb luck. The fact that Griff trusts me enough to tell me as much as he did about their work is an even bigger motivator.

In the blink of an eye, I'm straddling him. I have no idea if I did it myself or if he pulled me on top of him. Griff's hands grip my hips, holding me in place as if he's scared I'll run away.

"I really thought you hated me," I breathe, my eyes lifting to meet his. Griff's eyes are hazel, but where they should be brown, they're blue. It's the strangest eye color I've ever seen. Combined with his blond shoulder length waves, he's entrancing.

"Why would you think that?" he asks with a scoff, as if he wasn't nearly as big an ass to me as Brady when we met.

"To be fair, I think Nico is the only one who does like me," I admit.

"Elskede, I could never hate you. I promised Raj to protect you, and I will. I just wasn't prepared to meet you when we did," he says.

"That doesn't mean you like me. It just means you told my guardian that you would protect me. The whole thing is a lot, and I don't know how to deal with it." I pause, then figure if Raj and Amara trusted these guys enough to protect me, they should know what they're getting into.

"There are things I don't know, and there are things Amara and Raj didn't know. I'm terrified, but I feel like I can trust you, even though I have no idea why," I say.

He nods, but doesn't say anything. It's painfully obvious that he's waiting for me to continue. Closing my eyes, I inhale a deep breath, and let it all out. "My parents were killed the day I was born. That's all I know about them; besides they entrusted me to my guardians...who appear to have entrusted me to you guys."

My voice cracks, and Griff's hand rubs from its resting place on my hip up to my shoulder and back in slow strokes. The sensation is extremely distracting, but I know if he stops, I'll cry.

"I'm not a good person. Not really. I know that people are after me for my powers, but I don't completely understand why. I have a very specific moral code. It's like a defining line of what's right and wrong. Because of that, I've done some things. Honestly, the things I've done seem to contradict my beliefs, but it's all about justice. I do what I have to in order to protect people who can't protect themselves. I'm sorry...I'm not explaining this very well, and I'm rambling." I pause again and take a deep breath.

Griff's hand stops moving just above my ass, and I whimper. It's the most embarrassing sound I've ever made, and I want to dash back to Nico's closet because of it. His chuckle and smirk don't help me with that feeling, but his hand does start moving again. Just not in the direction I want it to. He rubs up and down my back again.

"Take a second. Just breathe. You don't have to tell me if you don't want to, or if you're not ready," he whispers. I shake my head, closing my eyes against the tears.

"I've killed people," I blurt.

Griff raises an eyebrow at me. "I know. We just cleaned up the bodies." Smart ass.

I shake my head again, and can't stop the tears this time. "No, before. It's something they didn't know about." I sniff and wipe at my eyes. "I was protecting people. Or at least that's what I told myself. I only went after predators; people who hurt other people. Rapists, domestic abusers, that kind of thing."

"Sounds like a noble cause," he agrees.

"I thought so, too. At first. But after a while, I realized that I was searching for them. Hunting them. And in hunting the monsters, I became one myself. I got lost in searching and taking them down. This is all my fault. If I had just suppressed that urge to kill, Amara and Raj—" I sob, unable to finish the thought. Guilt eats at me. Everything is my fault. I did this to my family.

Griff takes my face in his hands, forcing me to look at him. "No, Elskede, this isn't your fault. None of it. You were doing something to help people who needed it. There's no shame in that. Maybe the guys and I can help you train so you don't need to use your magic as much for it. Then you'll be harder to track."

My eyes go wide at his offer. Does this man really not care that I'm a cold-blooded killer? How is this possible?

Before I can respond to his kind words, he pulls me closer and presses his lips to mine. The kiss is tender, but heated. Griff's lips are both soft and demanding, claiming me in a way no one has before. My thoughts and fears melt away. Nothing else exists in this moment but him. I'm not even sure that I'm breathing right now.

His tongue brushes against my lips, and I part them with a desperate sigh. Griff fists his hand in my dark hair, and I grip his shoulders so tightly, I know he's going to have marks from my nails. As his tongue dances with mine, exploring and tasting, I barely realize that I'm grinding on his lap. Until my core brushes against his erection and he groans.

"Elskede, we need to slow down," he says against my lips. I nod and try to pull away. Griff tightens his hold on me, and trails open mouth kisses down my jaw and neck. Electricity zips through me, and I realize that I've felt this sensation before. It's the same thing that happened when I first touched Griff, both times. His lips, tongue, and teeth on my skin make it hard to focus on figuring out the electricity sensation.

BRADY

Nico stares at me blankly as we reenter the gala. I know he's pissed, and I understand why. "I'm not gonna talk about this now," I growl.

"I'm not finishing the job until you admit it," he argues.

"What difference will it make, Nico?"

"It'll explain why you're being such a dick, for one. And it will help us get on the same page about what's going to happen with this situation. Denying it won't help. I saw your face when you realized that she was in danger," he insists.

And he's right, denying it won't help. I'm just not ready to admit that she's my fated mate. Especially when my two best friends seem attached to her too. Are we supposed to share her? That seems weird, even to me.

"There's nothing to discuss, Nico. We need to get this job done. Unless you'd rather explain to Brynn why we agreed to it and then backed out?" Threatening him with Brynn isn't going to work, and I know it. Nico isn't scared of anything, much less the pink fluff that gives us our assignments.

He glares at me, and I wince. "If you just help me with this, we can sit down and talk about everything after. Okay? Please, Nico. Let's get the job done first."

His smirk elicits an involuntary growl from me, and I realize that I've lost the battle. No matter how much I try to deny it, he knows now that he's right. She's connected to all three of us. I start to wonder if it was a good idea to leave her alone with Griff. Surely, he won't make a move on her, right?

It doesn't really matter if he does. I can't focus on her with the job. It wouldn't be fair to pull someone so perfect into our darkness. No matter how strong the connection feels, we're going to have to let her go as soon as we know she's safe. It's ridiculous to think we can keep her with us, and keep her safe. Those ideas are way too contradictory to actually work.

I push those thoughts and feelings aside. We have to focus on the job. If we don't kill Jericho tonight, we'll risk Brynn sending someone else to do it, and to hunt us down. I can't allow that.

Scanning the room, it takes a few minutes to locate our prey. I gesture to Nico to get into position. Our plan won't work as smoothly without Griff, but I'm certain the two of us can handle it. How hard can it be to kill one man?

Nico and I subtly maneuver Jericho into place before I approach. A hand slams onto my chest before I can get close enough to speak to the target. "That's close enough," a gruff voice says.

"I'm just networking, man. What the hell?" I feign surprise, even though I expected to run into security. We just hadn't figured out which of the man's entourage was the muscle yet.

"Mr. J doesn't want to be bothered. He's enjoying his evening," the man says, his hand still pressed on my chest.

In any other situation, I would rip this guy's arm off and destroy him to get to my target. However, we were specifically instructed to not cause a scene at the gala. Who knows why Brynn decides these things, but with what we get paid, I can't argue.

"Listen, man. I don't want any trouble. You say your boss doesn't wanna network, that's fine by me. I'll go the other way. No harm, no foul, right?" I'm careful to keep my tone light but annoyed. I need this guy to believe that I don't like him touching me, but that I'm not after his boss.

"Then go the other way, and we won't have a problem," he growls, shoving me back. I close my eyes for a second and bite back my antagonistic response.

"Have a great night," I say as I walk backward away from the guy. Hopefully Nico has better luck getting close. This is why we need Griff. He's way better at talking his way past security, or entrancing them, or whatever. Hell, I don't even know the extent of my friends' powers. All I know is that the three of us can get any job done. I won't let that end tonight.

I lean against the wall near the bar, as close as I can get to where Jericho is without setting off his guard again. At this point, I'm pretending to watch the crowd and act as if I'm still annoyed at that guy's reaction to me. It's not a hard sell. I would rather have knocked him out and stomped his face than walking away. But the job is the job, and the client wants things done a certain way.

That doesn't mean this bear of a man won't somehow run into trouble after the job is complete. Once Jericho is dead, there will be no reason I can't have a conversation with this asshole and show him exactly what kind of trouble I'm capable of.

I drag my attention back to the room, searching out Nico. I know he saw me fail, and that he's moving on to Plan B. How he's going to get past this guard is beyond me. All I can do now is watch and wait for the signal that he needs me to intervene.

Nico approaches the bar, near Jericho. The guard steps over, but Nico dismisses him. I wonder what he says, but it really doesn't matter as long as he can get close to our target. We need to get him alone so we can take him out without causing a scene here.

Shock grips me when Nico walks past Jericho, completely ignoring the man. What the fuck is he doing? My friend sidles up to the bar and orders a drink. I'm confused and irritated until I see exactly what Nico is doing. By ignoring Jericho, he's bypassing the guards, and getting the target to come to him.

NICO

After watching Brady crash and burn in his attempt to get close to Jericho, I realize that I'm going to have to employ a completely different tactic. Approaching him directly isn't going to work, and could destroy our chances of finishing the job tonight. I definitely don't want Brynn coming after us. Not much scares me, but that particular Fae is terrifying. So pink and bubbly. A shudder runs through me at the thought. Well, that's not happening.

I'll just have to make Jericho come to me. The challenge there is that I'm not a teenage girl, or a pound of blow. As badly as I want this job done, I'm not confident we can complete it tonight. But I can't give up. If we fail, it will put all of us in danger, including Zola.

I spend a few minutes trying desperately to attract Jericho's attention, but he seems to only have eyes for the scantily clad women hanging on him. Fuck. This is not gonna happen tonight, and we'll have to deal with the fallout.

Locking eyes with Brady across the room, I shake my head. He nods, and walks outside. I should be glad that we're getting out of here without tipping Jericho off that we're after him. Instead, I'm pissed at myself for leaving Zola at the hideout alone when we came here earlier. If I had just insisted that we bring her, we could have completed the job by now and kept her safe at the same time.

Wishing I had a way to contact Brynn and explain the situation, I wait a beat and follow Brady out of the gala. We've never failed a mission before, and I don't want to admit defeat now. I approach my shifter friend, and see his thoughts all over his face. "Don't start. I know, okay? We'll get it figured out. We just need to do some recon and figure out where and when we can get to him," I insist.

"You'd better be right," Brady responds. "Otherwise, we're screwed and will be running from whoever Brynn sends after us." He's right. That vindictive Fae will probably send another crew to finish the job, and us. Fuck.

GRIFFIN

Elskede's secret is a lot to process. We were worried about bringing her into our world, and it appears that was unnecessary. I can't help thinking that she may be helpful to us in the mission we've already botched. If Brynn gives us a chance to complete it.

I want her more than I can stand. Pulling away and stopping this makes my cock ache. But she's not in the right headspace to bond with a fated mate right now. Especially when she doesn't even know that's what she's asking me to do. A permanent mate bond is something that can't be undone, and if it's not what she wants, we'd both be miserable trying to break it. I won't do that to her. I can't take advantage of her, knowing that it's not just me she's mated to. The guys and I haven't even discussed the situation yet. We're gonna have to, and soon.

"Elskede," I say again, dragging my lips from her skin. "We need to talk about this. The four of us." I know from her expression that she thinks I mean her secret, and while that is important, it's not my current concern.

"Do you think they'll want me to leave? I know I'm horrible, but maybe I can help you," she says quickly.

I close my eyes and press my forehead to hers. "I don't think that will be an issue. No one is going to ask you to leave. I just want everyone to understand the situation, and what's going to happen if we continue."

Her cheeks turn pink as she understands my meaning. "Oh, you mean this," she says, gesturing between us. "I, um..." she trails off, unsure of what to say.

"It's not exactly what you think. There are things you don't know yet, and it's not my place to tell you. I will say that moving forward with me, or Nico, or even Brady, isn't going to be easy."

Zola's face reddens more, and I suspect I know what she's thinking. "I'm not asking you to choose. I have no problem sharing with my friends. It's just a little more complicated than that, and we all need to talk before something happens that can't be undone. I understand that probably doesn't make sense right now, but it will."

"So, you're not rejecting me?" she asks, ducking her head to break eye contact.

I tilt her chin up with a finger so she's looking at me again. "Not at all. I promise we'll discuss it as soon as the guys get back, and you'll understand everything." I pull her close and rest her head on my chest. She relaxes against me, and I wonder if it will really be as easy as it seems in my mind. Zola's soft snores ease my mind a bit, and I settle in to wait for Nico and Brady to return.

Out of the corner of my eye, I notice the pink orb form. I turn toward it, careful to lay Zola down on the couch as I step in front of her. This can't be good. Maybe I can ignore it until the guys get back? That idea goes down the drain as it moves closer. I almost chuckle at the idea that the pink bubble is stalking me.

On the Run

ZOLA

Being dumped on the couch wakes me, but I don't say a word when Griff steps in front of me. I peer around him to see what's triggered this response. It looks like a shimmery pink bubble. How is this amazing warlock scared of bubbles? There must be more to it than I realize.

I watch, holding my breath, as the weird orb moves closer. Is it some kind of poison? Will it hurt Griff if it touches him? I have no way to know, but his panic is clear. The closer that thing gets, the more freaked out he is.

I spring to a sitting position, fling my hands out, and freeze the thing before it can attack. Griff stares at it, and I finally let out my breath. He turns to me, "How did you do that?" As if I've done something spectacular.

With a shrug, I answer, "I froze it. What the hell is that thing? Why are you so scared of it?" His face contorts and I can tell that he's trying to decide if he should tell me or not. Then I realize that it has to be related to their job. Before I can voice that question, Brady and Nico burst into the room.

"We have to go," Brady says. "Pack a single bag with what you absolutely need. I don't know if we can fix this or not, but we're gonna try."

Each of the guys darts off to follow Brady's order. I wait a moment, watching the frozen ball fight against my magic. Nico returns first, carrying his bag and mine. I forgot that I'd left it in his closet.

"Thank you," I say, reaching out for the bag. He drops it on the couch and drags me into his arms, holding me tightly against his chest.

"Please don't worry. We will protect you," he says against my hair.

"I'm not worried," I lie. "Besides, it looks like I can protect you, too. Even if I have no idea what I'm protecting you from." I know this isn't the time to discuss it, but I hope that they'll tell me once we're somewhere safe.

Nico leans down and captures my lips with his. Caught off guard, I gasp, and his tongue dips inside my mouth to explore. I melt against him, giving in to the desire that courses through me. Should I feel guilty that I was making out with Griff less than an hour ago? Maybe, but I can't focus on that right now. This kiss is nothing but raw passion, hot and fast. When he pulls away, a whimper escapes me.

My cheeks heat when I realize that he broke the kiss because Brady came into the room. "We don't have time for that right now. Come on, we have to go before the orb unfreezes. It's not like we're gonna be able to hide for long anyway. We need to get out of here and get a plan in place."

Is that a hint of jealousy? Brady doesn't even like me, why would he be jealous? Unless he's attracted to me, but for some reason it makes him angry. None of this makes sense, but I don't have time to analyze anyone's motives.

Griff is the last to return, and I'm surprised to find him empty-handed. "Pocket dimension," Nico whispers to me, as if that explains it. Before I can ask what he means, Griff waves his hands and a portal opens.

"Drop your bags in here. They'll be safe and we won't have to carry them," he explains as Brady and Nico set our bags inside. I guess that explains what a pocket dimension is.

That portal closes and another opens. Brady steps through and motions for us to follow. The shimmery pink orb breaks free of my ice, and starts zipping toward us. "Hurry up," Brady says, grabbing my arm and dragging me through the opening. Nico and Griff follow, and the magical doorway closes seconds before the bubble can force its way through.

"Where are we? What is going on? What the hell was that bubble thing, and why is it after us?" I ask, glaring at Brady, as if he'll attempt to avoid the questions.

He looks from Griff to Nico, then back to me. "This is the only safehouse we have that no one else knows about. We're hiding so we don't get killed for failing to complete our mission. And we're going to figure out a way to get the job done so the orbs and Fae don't keep hunting us down."

His answer doesn't really tell me much, but the fact that he walks away tells me that he's not really concerned with filling me in. I look at Griff, who shrugs and follows Brady. Nico shakes his head.

"So that's it? I don't need to know any more than that. I'm just supposed to trust you guys and go along with whatever even though I have no idea what's chasing us?" It's not like I have any other options, but it would be nice to get answers. Sadly, it doesn't look like that's gonna happen.

Nico's lack of response is disheartening, but I can't focus on that right now. I turn in a circle, checking out the room Griff brought us to. I have a dozen more questions I want to ask. Annoyance and frustration take over, causing me to walk away in the opposite direction Griff and Brady went. Nico doesn't follow me, so I assume I'm safe enough here.

Upon exploring the building, I realize that we're still somewhere in the city. I sense the river nearby, so this must be a different warehouse near the docks, even though there are no windows. After inspecting several rooms, I choose one for myself that has a lock on the door. The whole place appears to be furnished, and it looks like every bedroom has an en suite bathroom, so that's a plus.

GRIFFIN

"What the fuck happened?" I ask, following Brady when he storms away from Zola.

"We couldn't complete the job," he says, not bothering to stop. I keep following him until we get to the kitchen. This isn't the time to worry about food, but I guess Brady doesn't care that I want more information.

"So, now we're stuck hiding from Brynn? Is that your brilliant plan?" I snarl. "How exactly is that gonna work, B? That fucker can find anyone, anywhere, no matter how well the think they're hidden. You know they have to know we're here, right? This place isn't any safer than where we were."

"Look, man, I'm trying. Okay? If you're not gonna do anything to help, then shut the fuck up," he growls. I start to argue but he holds up a hand. "I mean it. If it's not a realistic suggestion, just shut up."

I stare at him for a moment, then realize he's right. I should be more worried about helping him figure out a way to keep our girl safe instead of trying to fight with him. Somehow, it's easier to let it go when I consider it that way. It's not totally Brady's fault that we fucked this job up. I know Nico and I are to blame as well.

"You're right, B. I'm sorry. It's not fair to blame you for everything. Let's see if we can come up with a way to finish the job so the guild doesn't come after us," I offer. At this moment, I have no idea how to make it happen, but I'm willing to brainstorm and see what we can come up with.

"Thanks. I appreciate that. We need to figure out where Jericho is and how to get to him. That's gonna be the hardest part. If we can corner him somewhere, we can take him out. I'm just not sure how to find him."

Brady's concerns make sense, and it's not like we can contact Brynn for help. "Wait. Doesn't Nico know a hacker? Couldn't they help us find Jericho?"

My shifter friend turns to stare at me. "That could actually work. Get Nico on that, and I'll arrange to get some supplies for us." Brady walks away without another thought.

Once Brady is gone, I head back to find Nico. With any luck, his hacker friend will be able to pin down Jericho's location and we'll be able to handle the mission and get back in Brynn's good graces.

NICO

When Zola walks away, I consider following. I know she's safe here, so there's no reason for stalking. Besides, I can send my shadows to keep an eye on her and they'll report back if she gets in danger.

My shadows also show me the bonds between Zola and my friends. Even if they haven't realized yet. I'm still considering the idea of the four of us being together when Griff walks in.

"What's up?" I ask, noticing his frown.

"Do you think your hacker friend can find Jericho for us?" he asks, not bothering with a greeting.

"You know I'm not actually friends with the hacker, right? It's one of her lovers that I grew up with. But yeah, I can contact Will and see if his lady will help us," I answer, knowing that pointing out the semantics will drive Griff crazy.

"Fine, fuck, whatever. Just do it. Brady is arranging supplies. We need to find Jericho and get this handled. Where is Zola?" Griff's attitude grates on me, but I let it slide. We're all stressed right now, and the last thing we need is to be fighting with each other.

I point in the direction she went, then pull out my phone to call Will. Even using our secure lines here is risky, but if I want to find our target, I'm gonna have to do it. There's no other way to get in touch. Taking a deep breath, I dial the number and wait.

"Nico? Are you okay?" Will's voice fills the air and I breathe a sigh of relief.

"Well, if you've heard about it, then I'm guessing we're not okay. I need your help. Or rather, your girl's help, if you can talk her into it," I start.

"We'll do whatever we can to help you fix this. Brynn even knows exactly what happened, and is still being a douche about it. Em is pissed, so I know she'll be in. What do you need?" he asks.

"Jericho's location and the easiest way to get to him. We're not asking you guys to do the job; we'll take care of that. We just lost him and don't have any leads on where to start. If we can locate him and get the job done, Brynn will call off the dogs, so to speak."

"Definitely. Send me what you've got on him, and I'll get back with you as soon as Em finds what you need. Stay safe," Will says as he disconnects the call. I shoot him a text with all the info we have on Jericho, including the details of how we fucked up the job. I know Will isn't gonna judge us, and if anyone understands needing to stand by your girl, it's him.

I despise playing the waiting game, so instead of dwelling on what's gone wrong, I decide to do some training and worry about what I can do to fix it. My shadows are an extension of myself, and my magical ability allows me to use them as if they were my limbs. It's not quite like being in two places at once, but it's pretty close.

Dropping to the floor, I lean against the wall and draw my legs up in front of me. With my eyes closed, I focus on the shadowy tendrils that flow from me. In this meditative state, I use the darkness to spy for me.

BRADY

I walk away from Griff intending to secure supplies, but wind up following a sweet scent I can't quite name. Something about it draws me in and entrances me. I can't help but track it. Opening a door, I understand why. Zola sits on the bed in the middle of the room, staring at the door.

"What happened?" she asks, clearly on the verge of panic.

"Nothing. I just wondered which room you'd chosen. I'm going to arrange supplies, and needed to know if there was anything you wanted." I stand there, staring at her as if she's the one who's invaded my privacy. Ignoring the fact that I walked into her room without even a courtesy knock, she scrunches her face in thought and stares at the ceiling for a minute.

Bringing her eyes back to mine, she blushes. "I'd really like some chocolate, and bottled spring water. If that's not too much trouble. I don't want to put you out." The sincerity in her voice nearly breaks me. I want nothing more than to rush over and drag her into my arms. But I can't let that happen. I cannot afford to get distracted. Griff and Nico did, and look where we are now. This girl may be special, but she's not mine.

Even as I have the thought, my leopard growls in my mind. I know the truth of the situation, but I'm not ready to accept it. I can't. If I do, it could cost us everything.

I realize suddenly that I've been standing here staring at her, and I haven't responded to what she said. "It's no problem, really. Chocolate and spring water. I think I can make that happen." I wonder what else she'd like, but don't push. I can get one of my contacts to find a soft blanket and cozy pillow to make her more comfortable here. It's not like she'll know it was my idea.

"Did you need anything else?" she asks, staring back at me. I can't tell if it's hope or annoyance in her eyes. Neither one is welcome right now, so it doesn't matter. I have to shut this down before either of us get the wrong idea.

"That was it. I'll let you know when the supplies get here. Don't go wandering the halls by yourself. There could be traps," I warn as I back out the door and pull it closed behind me. Yes, I'm immature and an asshole. There are no traps, and there's no reason she shouldn't be out wandering the compound. Everything is secure, and we're far enough underground that no one will know we're here. But I'd rather scare her into staying put so I don't have to worry about running into her.

Shoving the guilt away, I walk back down the hall the way I came, stopping at my bedroom to make the calls I need to for supplies. I should have asked if she had any food allergies or preferences, but that would have given away too much.

ZOLA

Brady barging into my room startles me. I'm half scared he's gonna tell me I have to leave because I led the pink orbs or Fae or whatever to them again. It doesn't matter that none of this is really my fault. He's pissed at me, and I know it. What I can't figure out is why he hates me so much but looks at me like he wants to eat me up. Or out, I don't know. He's hot, but a total dick. I bet he has a big one, too.

No, I am not sitting here thinking about Brady's dick. He doesn't like me, so I don't like him. As if it's that easy to turn desires and feelings off. I laugh at myself, then wonder where the other guys went. I don't mind being alone, but this whole situation has been a lot to handle, especially with Amara and Raj being killed the way they were. I'm struggling to hold it together; more so when I'm alone than when someone is around to distract me.

A few minutes after Brady leaves, I feel a sense of comfort wrap around me, as if someone is hugging me. I look around, but no one is in the room with me. When I look down, I notice that I'm surrounded by shadows. Nico. I take comfort in him checking on me, even if he pissed me off earlier. My emotions are all over the place, and my attraction to these men does not help me with processing my guardians' deaths.

I can't sit around here forever, waiting to see what happens next. I have to prepare for whatever the guys will need me to do. I'm responsible for this situation, so I need to help fix it. It doesn't matter that I don't fully understand it all. I know that I kept them from focusing on their target, and I need to stop getting in the way.

I don't know how to find the man they're supposed to kill, but once they locate him, I have ways that I can take him out so they don't have to worry about missing a chance again. Lying there on the bed, I let my mind wander to all the ways I could kill a man without anyone realizing it was me. I don't enjoy knowing that my darkness is almost equal to these men. They're murderers, after all. No, not murderers, assassins. They kill for money, not for justice. But why can't it be both? Maybe it is, and I just don't know about it yet.

With ideas of killing bad men and making the world a better place, I start to doze off. It makes me wonder what kind of monster I really am if I can fall asleep to thoughts of torture and death. So far, I've been able to control my dark side. Will it last?

Running Away

ZOLA

At some point after I fall asleep, the nightmares start again. No matter how realistic it is, a part of me knows it's a dream, and that I'm safe. That doesn't stop me from screaming and waking up drenched in sweat. I have no idea how long I've been asleep, or where the guys are. I bolt upright in bed, panting, with tears streaming down my face.

The door slams open and before I can process what's happening, I'm in Nico's arms and Griff is standing in the doorway. "What happened? Where did they go?" Griff asks as Nico gently rubs my back and presses my face to his chest.

"It was a nightmare. No one broke in," Nico says quietly. I wonder for a moment if he's telling Griff or me.

Dragging in a few deep breaths, I relax against Nico. A moment later, I realize that Griff is on the other side of me, and they're caging me in. I should object. The right thing to do would be to deny the attraction and push them both away, but I can't. Being sandwiched between them should be awkward, but it feels like the most natural thing ever.

"Have you been having nightmares a lot?" Griff asks, pressing a kiss to my temple when I turn so I can see them both.

"Almost every night since it happened," I answer, knowing that they'll understand what *it* is.

"Well, you don't have to be alone anymore if you don't want to, Dewdrop," Nico says, glancing from me to Griff and back. "We're here, and we'll stay with you as long as you need."

I hate the idea that I need them, but he's right. I can't be alone. Not yet. I have to figure out how to deal with this huge loss and what I can do to move on. I know that staying here isn't an option, even if the guys say they promised my guardians they would keep me safe. But maybe I can allow myself some comfort, temporarily, until I'm ready to be on my own.

"Thank you both," I say, leaning against the pillow between them. Nico brushes my hair off my face, trailing his fingers along my jaw. I let my eyes flutter closed and tilt my chin slightly. I want him to kiss me. If I'm being honest, I want them both to. I should pull away, but I don't.

Soft lips gingerly slide against mine, sending a shiver down my spine. I lean into it, trying to deepen the kiss, but whichever guy instigated it pulls away. Cold air replaces the warmth of their bodies against me, and my eyes fly open.

Nico and Griff stare at me, as if they're trying to figure something out. My face scrunches in confusion. "What's wrong?" I ask, a million reasons for their rejection racing through my head.

"We can't take advantage of you, Dewdrop," Nico says. I thread my fingers through his, then take Griff's hand in my other, doing the same.

"How are you taking advantage of me if this is what I want?"

"Because you don't understand what you're getting into," Griff answers.

"What are you talking about? I know what you guys do, and you know my secret. I'm attracted to you, and I thought you guys wanted me. What more is there to know?" I push harder, annoyed at the hot/cold thing going on now.

"Elskede, before things go too far, you need to know what will happen if we claim you," Griff says.

"Claim me? Like I'm dry cleaning? Or a lost pet? You've got to be kidding me." I release their hands and push myself off the bed. "You know what? Forget it. I'm not property, and I don't want to be *claimed.* Thank you for comforting me after my nightmare, but I think you should go now." I turn my back on the two of them, facing the door so I'll know when they leave.

"Dewdrop, please," Nico begs. His tone makes me want to cave to his desires, but I refuse to let someone think they can own me. If my guardians taught me anything, it was my own worth.

I shake my head in response, refusing to look at him. "Just go," I whisper. I wrap my arms around my stomach, hoping that they leave before my tears manage to escape. With a sigh, both men walk past me to the door, each one pausing for a moment as if trying to decide if touching me is a good idea.

I will not cry in front of them. Not over this. I refuse to let them know how much power they actually have over me. The moment the door closes, I flip the lock on it and head to the en suite bathroom, grabbing my backpack on the way. I don't have much, but I can at least change my clothes after a shower.

Since I know more sleep is out of the question, spending some time in the water will help relax me. It's not the same as swimming in a lake, but any connection to the elements is better than none. Sitting on the floor of the shower, I finally let the tears fall as the water cascades around me. My grief consumes me, and I sit under the water until it runs cold and my tears run out. I can't stay here, even if it's the safest place I've been in a while.

Feeling more alone than ever, I dry myself slowly, comb out and braid my hair, then get dressed. Brady told me to stay in this room, but I need to move. I can't just sit here and wait for them to tell me we need to leave again. Piling everything back into my backpack, I close it, tossing it over my shoulder as I head out the door.

I walk down the hall wondering where the exit is. I haven't really explored this place, and have no idea where here even is. All I know is that I can't sit in that room any longer, and I'm not about to run to the two guys who both rejected me and tried to treat me like property.

BRADY

I turn a corner, heading to my room and slam into Zola. Pulling her to my chest to keep her from hitting the floor, I notice she has her backpack on, and she's clearly upset.

"Are you going somewhere?" I ask. What's spooked her into running?

"I have to get out of here. Don't worry about me. I'll be fine. I can take care of myself, really," she insists.

I shake my head, not releasing her when she pushes against my chest. "I made a promise, and I'm not about to go back on my word now."

"I get that, but I have to go. I can't stay here," she insists again.

Okay, clearly this isn't gonna be easy. "Please, just tell me what happened to upset you, and if we can't fix it, I'll escort you to the door." I can tell that she doesn't want to, but she nods. "I'm guessing you don't really want to do that right here?"

She nods, and I scoop her up into my arms. "Wait," she says.

"It's okay. We're going somewhere private to talk. No one is going to hurt you," I promise her. Then I start to wonder if someone already had. If these dumbasses already managed to chase her off, I might be working on my own again once I kill them. I head back to my room, hoping that Zola will talk to me, and that I can do something about whatever has her so upset.

Once inside my room, I close the door but don't lock it. I don't want her to feel trapped here. Setting her down on the overstuffed armchair in the corner, I fight the urge to pull her back into my arms and sit with her. I am not going to accept this mate bond. I can't afford to.

"Okay, can you tell me what happened?" I push, grabbing two bottles of water from my mini fridge and handing one to her. Zola twists it open and takes a gulp before answering.

"Griff and Nico," she starts, then shakes her head.

"Did they hurt you, Kotik?"

She shakes her head again. "Not physically. I, I don't know. This is awkward. I should just leave," she finishes, her cheeks stained pink.

"Did they try to force you into something you didn't want?" I hate this line of questioning, and would be shocked if her answer was yes, but I have to know. If either of my friends tried to manipulate or use brute force to claim her, I'll kill them. I may not be a good man, but harming innocents or children is where I cross the line.

Tears fill her eyes, and I can see how hard she's fighting to keep them from falling. "It's okay, Kotik. Your tears don't make you weak. Please tell me what they did so I can punish them for hurting you." I don't recognize my own voice because it's so soft and gentle. That's not me; it's not who I am.

"I—please don't fight with them about it. I've had enough fighting for one day." She pauses for a moment. "It's my fault anyway. They started talking about claiming me as if I were property and it pissed me off. I'm not helpless, stupid, or something to own. If they can't see that, I can't stay here."

Those dumbasses. I understand now why she's trying to leave. If they fucked up explaining a mating claim to her, they deserve to think she's taken off. Maybe I'll let them worry for a while.

"Do you want to get back at them for being idiots?" I ask. When she nods hesitantly, I continue. "I have an idea, but it involves you staying here and hiding from them. Are you interested?"

The smile she gives me could light up the darkest room, and I can't help giving her an equal smile back. After discussing the details of my idea, and Zola making a few changes, we decide that we're good to go.

"You know, I didn't even think you liked me," she says. "And now here we are moving in together." Her laugh is contagious, and I realize that I'm desperate to hear it again as soon as it stops. Oh, no. I may have gotten myself in trouble here.

"It's not that I don't like you," I explain, wondering if I'm making things better or worse by admitting this. "It's that I can't afford any distractions. The job I do, that we do, is very time sensitive. Having a mate bond is a similar kind of commitment. Of course I like you; you're beautiful, intelligent, and caring. But I'm not ready for a mate, and I don't think you are either."

She glares at me, and I force myself to continue. "Are you ready to feel like you would sacrifice everything to protect someone else?" The question throws her off, and I wait for her to recover.

"I hadn't thought of it like that. Do you think that's what Nico and Griff were trying to explain when they compared me to their dry cleaning?" she asks, her cheeks rosy again.

"It's possible. Some people have trouble focusing on hunting down the right words when they have a beautiful woman in their arms. I'm guessing that's what was wrong with those two idiots. And I'm not saying that you should forgive them; at least not right away. Make them work for it. But don't count them out completely because of one conversation, okay?" Why am I defending my friends to my fated mate? It would be different if I was certain she'd be into a polyamorous relationship, but I can't even ask that, because I've only known her for a few days now.

ZOLA

Hiding from my problems is not how I was raised, but it does make me feel better. Especially when Brady brings dinner to me and explains how the other two are searching for me everywhere. After we eat, he goes into the en suite to shower, and I realize that I may have made a mistake agreeing to this arrangement.

"Um, Brady?" I ask from my seat on the oversized chair, when he comes back into the room.

"Yeah, Kotik, what's up?" he answers, scrubbing at his damp hair with a towel. I can't help being a little distracted by the fact that he only appears to be wearing a thin pair of shorts. When I don't answer right away, he stops and turns to face me. "What's wrong?"

"Where am I going to sleep?"

"You can sleep in the bed, of course. I wouldn't put you on the floor," he says with a smirk. I still don't think he understands what I'm asking. So, I try again.

"And where are *you* going to sleep?" I raise my eyebrows at him and wait for my meaning to sink in.

"Oh. Well, I was planning to sleep in the bed, too." His cheeks redden with his response, and I can't stop the laugh that rolls out of me.

"I didn't think you wanted a mate," I reply. I intend to sound teasing, but it comes out sounding more serious.

"Well, I mean, if I sleep somewhere else, the guys might notice and realize that I'm hiding you in here. If I'm here, they have no reason to come snooping around," he answers quickly.

"And you wouldn't make a man sleep on the floor in his own room, would you?" He fakes shock at his question and I shake my head.

"Can you promise to stay on your side and keep your hands to yourself?" I ask, wondering if I'm crazy for considering this.

He trails a finger over his bare chest in an X motion. "Cross my heart. I will not touch you in any way unless you ask me to." Something in his tone makes me wonder if he wants me to ask him. And something in his eyes makes me wonder if I want to ask him. Fuck. This is a bad idea. But the alternative is going back to my room and letting the other two off the hook already.

Since I don't like the idea of giving up my torture just yet, I decide to suck it up and continue this game of chicken that I'm playing with Brady. "Okay. I can handle that," I answer. My heart races and my throat feels like I've swallowed the desert, but I refuse to let him know I'm feeling intimidated.

Yes, this shifter is cranky and blunt. But he's never done anything to intentionally hurt me. Of course, I've only known him for a few days, but something tells me that I'm as safe here as I can be. Given everything that's happened, security is all I can ask for. And being in the room with a trained assassin is probably safer than sleeping alone, right?

For the second time tonight, I start to question my sanity at agreeing to this, when we climb into bed next to each other. "You're gonna sleep in your clothes?" he asks.

"I don't exactly have a full wardrobe with me, so yeah," I answer, settling in under the blanket.

"If you need something to sleep in, I can loan you a shirt. It'll be huge on you, but might be more comfortable than what you're wearing," he offers.

I'm not sure if I should take him up on it or not. On one hand, I'd be way more comfortable. On the other, I'd be wearing a lot fewer clothes. I consider my options for a moment, then decide that if I'm doing this, I might as well be all in.

"A shirt would be great, thanks." I toss the covers back and climb out of bed when he hands me a t-shirt. I change in the bathroom, hoping that maybe he'll already be asleep when I get back. Since the lights are still on, and he's sitting up in bed staring at the bathroom door, I realize that's not gonna happen.

Brady's breath hitches when I walk out of the bathroom. "What is it?" I ask, wondering if I've somehow upset him, or if he's rethinking this situation too.

"Nothing is wrong, Kotik. I just wasn't prepared to see you in my clothes, that's all. It has unexpected side effects on a man. But I'm okay, really. I won't go back on my word, either," he vows.

I'm not sure if I'm relieved or annoyed at his statement. And the way he's looking at me, I'm not sure which he is, either. "Maybe I should just sleep in the chair?"

Brady shakes his head. "Not a chance. Come on, let's get some sleep. We've got torture for the guys scheduled for tomorrow, remember?" He pats the bed beside him and I slowly walk over.

This situation is awkward, but I'm more comfortable than I should be. What is it about these men that puts me at ease, even when they look at me like I could be their dinner? I'm certain Raj and Amara would not approve of any of this, even though they're the ones who set these guys up to protect me. And it's not like I can call them and ask, anyway.

That thought stabs a pain through my heart. I turn away from Brady as I fight back the tears. Guilt eats at me, and I wish I could change things. My guardians didn't deserve to die like that.

"Get some rest, Kotik. We're gonna start training with your magic tomorrow. You have to be able to protect yourself."

I sniffle when I nod, and Brady wraps an arm around me, pulling me to rest my head on his chest. "This isn't me breaking my word. It's me comforting you because you lost your family. If you're not okay with it, just tell me." I shake my head and snuggle against him, letting his heartbeat lull me to sleep.

Oops

ZOLA

I WAKE IN A haze, warmth surrounding me like I've never felt before. Strong arms hold me close to a hard chest covered with soft hair. I release a sigh of contentment as I trail my fingers along his abs. I wonder if Brady will change our arrangement after sleeping so closely last night. Or will he be stubborn and insist that I ask him to touch me the way I want?

Maybe I should just ask him to touch me. That would ease the ache in my core. But would he want that? Brady made it pretty clear last night that he doesn't want a mate, even though he knows that we're fated. I don't even understand what that means. It's not like anyone explained fated mates to me. And since I may have overreacted when Griff and Nico tried, I'm at a little bit of a disadvantage here.

I trail my fingers down his abs again, stopping at the waistband of his shorts. A groan rumbles through his chest next to my ear, and a chill washes over me. Tracing my fingers back and forth at the edge of the fabric, I bite my lower lip to hold back my own groan of frustration.

"Kotik, if you keep doing that, this may turn into something besides sleep," Brady grumbles. "So, unless you're prepared to ask for what you want, you should stop now."

Well, that answers that question. "What if I know what I want? And what if I want to show you instead of using words?" My tone is coy and flirty, sounding nothing like me.

"Are you proposing an adjustment to my promise, then? Or do you just plan to torture me by not allowing me to touch you?" My breath hitches at his words, shivers of promised pleasure racing down my spine.

"I'm not sure yet," I admit, dipping my fingertips just below the fabric of his waistband. "Maybe I want you to take back that promise altogether." I tilt my head to look at him, watching his eyes go wide.

"I will not take advantage of you. If you want me, I need to hear it. And I need you to agree that this can't be anything more than sex. I can't give you anything else." His words sting, but my body is throbbing with the thought of him touching me. Besides, who wants to promise forever to someone they just met?

"I don't need fancy words or promises. I need to be fucked. By someone who isn't gonna be too worried about hurting me to give me the pleasure I desire," I admit. The blunt statement isn't something I'd usually be comfortable with, but I understand that he needs to know exactly what I want.

Brady smirks, then flips on top of me, grinding his erection against my core. "Do you feel what you do to me, Kotik?"

I gasp at the friction of our contact, wanting more. Nodding, I pull him down to me and press my lips to his. "I need more," I breathe against his mouth.

Without another word, Brady rubs himself against me again, taking my lips with his as his hands slide from my hips to my waist, under his t-shirt. His rough hands against my soft skin make me tremble. He pauses for a moment, and I grab the hem of the shirt and pull it over my head, leaving nothing between us but his shorts and my panties.

Brady growls, a deep sound low in his throat. There's something primal about it, and for a half-second, I wonder if this was a bad idea. Then his lips are on my skin, trailing from my jaw down my neck to tease my nipples to stiffness. I moan and pant his name as he drives me higher with only his mouth moving on me.

Digging my fingers into his short hair, I encourage him to continue. I'm desperate to feel his hands all over me, teasing and stroking me until I can't take anymore. "Please," I beg.

He smiles against my skin, dragging kisses back up until his mouth is on mine again. With a jerk of his hand against my hip, my panties shred to pieces. Brady's fingers stroke around my core, teasing me by touching all around where I want him. Just when I think I'm going to scream from it, he slides one finger inside me and flicks my clit with his thumb.

I cry out, bucking my hips at him, trying to force him to go faster; to give me more. But Brady doesn't stop his slow caress, sliding his finger in and out of me while stroking my clit with his thumb. I growl at him, refusing to beg more. He has the nerve to laugh at my reaction to his torture.

"What's wrong, Kotik? Am I hurting you?" he laughs.

"This is torture, Brady. I need more," I snarl. My hips chase his hand as he withdraws from me. His hand fists in my hair, tilting my head back so he can suck on my neck. I feel the scrape of his teeth at the same moment he thrusts two thick fingers inside of me. Crying out, I lift myself to meet his fingers as they slam into me over and over.

When I'm so worked up that I feel like I'll explode, he pulls away again. "What the fuck?" I ask, pushing my damp hair off my face.

He smirks at me, licks my juices from his fingers, and pulls off his shorts, freeing his cock. Oh. My. That thing is bigger than I expected. Not that I spent a lot of time the past few days thinking about it. Of course, I didn't. That would have been really inappropriate, right?

I reach for him, but he grabs both my wrists and holds them with one hand. "If you touch me right now, that will be the end of this. And I don't know about you, but I'm not ready for that yet," he warns.

My eyes go wide and I shake my head, relaxing my arms in his hold. He spreads my legs and settles between them, taking a deep breath and closing his eyes for a moment. When he opens them again, his eyes glint amber, and I wonder if that's his beast clawing its way to the surface.

Could he lose control and shift while we're in the middle of having sex? I hadn't thought to ask about that before we started. And I've never been with a shifter before. I've only had sex twice, and both times were with human men I met at frat parties. Brady is so much more than either of them.

The ache in my core builds again, and I whimper. He looks into my eyes and slowly strokes his cock against my slick opening. Another whimper escapes me, and he smirks again. "Please, Brady, I need you," I pant, feeling like I'm going to die if he doesn't fuck me now.

With a possessive growl, he thrusts inside of me, filling me to the hilt. I cry out; partly because he's huge and it hurts, and partly because it also feels so amazing. Brady pauses for a moment, then slowly starts moving. He drags himself back, pulling almost all the way out of me before slamming back down into my greedy pussy. With grunts and moans of en-couragement coming from both of us, we manage to find a pace that's fast and hard enough for both of us to enjoy the ride. I know I'll be sore for a while after, but I can't find the ability to care right now.

He thrusts into me, over and over, pushing me toward an-other climax. My body coils like a snake about to strike, and

I feel like I'm going to pass out. Crying out his name as my orgasm takes me over the edge, coaxing Brady to follow, I feel something warm and tingly snap into place between us.

My half-closed eyes snap open and lock with his. "What the fuck is that?" I ask. The shock on his face mirrors my own.

"Fuck," he answers as he finishes filling me with his release. My body shudders and dread sets in, even though I feel safer and more sated than I ever have.

"That's not...it can't be...we didn't," I can't form coherent sentences, but manage to crawl out from under Brady and run to his bathroom. Before he can follow me, I lock the door and flip on the shower. I wash myself with his shampoo and soap, then turn the water up as hot as I can stand. Steam fills the room, and I drop to my knees in the shower stream.

That's what Nico and Griff wanted me to understand before we did anything. Why did I get so upset about them trying to warn me? I should have listened, then I wouldn't have bonded with a man who doesn't want me.

I don't know how long I sit in the shower, letting the hot water and steam surround me. I refuse to move until the water starts to go cold. When I step out of the shower, I dry myself and wrap the towel around me, grabbing a second one for my hair. With it twisted up off my neck, something catches my attention in the mirror.

What the fuck is that? I step closer to take a look. There are teeth marks on my throat, and they're not shallow. It looks like a predator sank their fangs into me. How did I not feel that? Did Brady bite me while we were having sex? I bring my fingers up to touch the wound, but it doesn't hurt. It's warm and tingly like the feeling that passed between us when we climaxed.

Shit. This is an even bigger mess. I just accidentally mate bonded with a man—a shifter—who doesn't want a mate. I don't know anything about mate bonds. Can we take it back? Are we stuck with each other forever now? Does it matter that I wasn't trying to bond with him? I have so many questions and know that I won't get any answers if I stay locked in the bathroom.

I dress quickly in the clothes I wore yesterday, toweling off my hair and running my fingers through it before hanging up the towels and leaving the bathroom. Brady is sitting on the bed in nothing but his shorts, staring at the door when I walk through.

"We should talk about this," I say, pulling my hair back to show him the mark.

"I didn't mean to," he starts, but I hold up a hand to stop him.

"I know. But you did, and here we are. What does it mean? Because I'm pretty sure it's not just a normal bite," I stare at him as guilt spreads across his face. "You claimed me, didn't you?"

He hangs his head for a moment. "I didn't intend to, but yes, it looks like my animal instincts took over and I claimed you. And it feels like you claimed me too, but I'm not sure how."

I shake my head. "I want you to know that I didn't plan this. You said you didn't want a mate, and I agreed with you. It has to be a partnership with two or more willing participants."

He nods, standing up and reaching out to take my hands in his. "Neither of us planned this, but we're going to have to figure it out. We're connected now. There's no way to reverse it. I'm so sorry." He pulls me into his arms and holds me tightly against his chest.

BRADY

The moment our bond snaps into place, I know I've fucked up. As much as I never wanted a mate, I'm drawn to Zola, and can't regret what's happened. At the same time, I'm pissed because I wasn't more careful. Now we're stuck with each other, and I don't know how to fix this.

I can't decide if I'm more pissed at myself or irritated at her for putting me in this position. I stare at the bathroom door the entire time she's in there, wondering how I'm going to handle this. When she comes out and starts asking questions, my first instinct is to comfort her.

Before I know what I'm doing, I pull her into my arms and hold her close. I have no idea what I'm going to do now, but I know there's no way to nullify a mate claim. Even though it's not what I ever thought I wanted, I'm not sure I would break it if I could. But how do I tell her that?

"I don't completely understand what this means for us, or in general, but if there's nothing we can do to make it stop or get rid of it, I guess we'll have to make it work," she says. My heart aches at her words, but then I realize that's not my pain I'm feeling. She's feeling guilty for essentially "trapping" me. This girl doesn't understand anything about mate bonds or how they're formed and thinks she's done something wrong.

"Kotik, there is nothing for you to feel guilty about," I assure her.

"But you didn't want this, and now you have no choice," she answers, burying her face in my chest. I know my scent is calming her, even if she doesn't realize what's happening.

"I don't blame you. Or me. I blame fate for putting us in this situation. It was inevitable that we'd claim each other given our proximity. Honestly, it was just a matter of time," I say.

Does she believe me? No idea, but the guilt wanes, and her breathing slows. At least she's beginning to calm down. Now I just have to figure out how to keep the guys from discovering our little problem.

"Do you still want to torture the guys for upsetting you?" I ask, hoping she'll say yes, so I have an excuse to keep her all to myself for a few days. I shake my head, wondering where that sudden desire sprang from.

Zola pulls away from me, walks over to the chair in the corner and sits down, pulling her knees up to rest her chin on them. "I don't know. I realize now that they were probably just trying to prevent what just happened with us." She smiles at me, but it holds more sadness than joy. "I think I might have overreacted because it embarrassed me. I assumed that they didn't want me instead of listening to what they had to say."

Before I can respond, my door shakes as someone starts pounding against it. "Brady! Zola is missing. We need your help to find her," Griff calls.

I exchange a look with my mate and she shrugs. "They're going to find out eventually. I think we should just own it."

Her words make me smile. Whether she understands the bond or not, she isn't ashamed of me, or of our claiming each other. It might make things awkward with the guys, but they'll get over it. Especially when they realize I'm not standing in their way. If Zola wants all three of us, I'll do whatever I can to make it happen.

I nod at her, then pull the door open. The guys rush in, talking over each other, until they see Zola. Both of my friends freeze, staring at her.

"Did you—?" Nico starts, cutting off when his eyes meet hers.

"No, that's not possible," Griff replies, "Is it?"

"If you're referring to the mating bond between Zola and myself, yes, it is possible. Yes, it happened. No, it was not a conscious decision on either of our parts. I do believe we've decided to try and make the best of it," I answer, gesturing to her to back me up.

"He's right. I owe you both an apology. I overreacted, thinking you were rejecting me, when I should have listened and let you explain. I hope you can forgive me," she says, lowering her eyes to the floor.

"Dewdrop, you have nothing to apologize for. We should have approached the subject with a bit more finesse, and better timing. We're sorry for pushing you away," Nico says, kneeling on the floor in front of her and taking one of her hands.

Zola lifts her eyes to meet his, tears streaming down her face. It takes every ounce of self-control I have to stop myself from walking over and tearing her away from him. I know that won't help the situation, since I'm almost certain my friends are fated to her as well. We're going to have to get used to sharing, and there's no better time than now to start.

"Have you heard back from your hacker?" I ask, allowing myself to pull the subject away from their connection. Just because I'm not fighting it, that doesn't mean I'm ready to hand her over to them yet.

"He's talking to her and they'll let us know if they can help," Nico says, turning his attention back to me. "Do you want to explain what happened here?"

"Not particularly. You already know how mate bonds work, so don't pretend that you need us to walk you through it," I answer with a smirk. "Unless you're asking for pointers, then I'm happy to help." It's a low blow and I know it, but I can't help myself.

TRAINING

NICO

Since Brady and Zola completed their mate bond, things are tense between the four of us. Griff and I are still drawn to her, and she seems interested. It's a complicated situation without the reminder of Brynn and the Fae hunting us down for not completing our contract.

The hardest transition for all of us has been Brady's mood swings. He's possessive, growling at us for getting too close to his mate; then standoffish because he claims he didn't want a mate in the first place. Poor guy is so confused that he doesn't know which way is up, and if it wasn't so annoying, it would be hilarious.

While we wait for Will to get back to me, we're focusing on training Zola to control her power and fight without it. The idea of letting her fight against anything makes me a little crazy, but I know the three of us won't always be able to protect her.

Griff tosses a fireball a little too close, and Brady tackles him. "Are you trying to kill her?" he growls.

Before I can cross the room to intervene, Zola sends Brady flying across the room with a gust of air. "Stop." The command freezes him as he climbs to his feet. She cuts him off before he can respond. "I mean it. Griff and Nico are helping me train. They can't go easy on me, and they can't worry if I'll get hurt. I have to learn to defend myself and control my magic. If you can't behave yourself while you watch, then you need to go."

Brady snarls, fighting his shift. Then Zola surprises us all by crossing the room and pressing her lips to his. "I'm okay. I can do this. Please let me learn."

He relaxes and nods, taking a step backward and leaning against the wall. I've never seen Brady bend to anyone else's will like that before. Griff and I exchange a look before turning back to Zola.

"Maybe we should take a break," Griff offers, acknowledging Brady's outburst. Zola gives him a dirty look, then focuses on me.

"You really wanna stop training because the big cat can't control his overprotective urges?" she asks.

"I know it's frustrating, but he just wants to keep you safe. It's a bond thing," I say.

She throws up her hands, muttering to herself about men, and walks away. Once she's out of the room, Griff and I set our laughter free, pulling more growls from Brady.

"You guys are dicks. You were attacking her like that to get me riled up. Admit it," he says.

"Of course we were. You did the thing we all wanted to, and now you have to suffer for it," Griff laughs. I nod thoughtfully. It's too bad she won't let Griff or I close enough to claim her, but I understand that she's not ready yet. Getting used to having someone else's feelings in your head has to be a lot.

My phone rings, and I step away from the guys to answer.

"Nico, it's Will. Em has what you need. I'll send the location over along with the rest of what she got. This isn't gonna be easy, though. Jericho is heavily guarded," he says, not bothering with a greeting or a pause until he's finished.

"We appreciate the info, and the help. We're not expecting easy, especially after the way we messed it up twice already. We just need to get it done as soon as possible," I answer.

"You need to make sure it's done before midnight tonight. I know that's not much time, but Brynn isn't going to hold back if the job isn't finished today. They've already reached out to us for clean up, but with a caveat that you have until 12:01 AM to get it taken care of. As of that point, we're up, and you guys become part of the job," Will explains.

Fuck, this is bad. Even with the few days' worth of training we've been able to give Zola, I don't think she's ready for this. But we can't leave her behind. Brady won't let us, and we wouldn't feel safe leaving her anyway. Having less than twelve hours to plan and execute a job isn't ideal, especially with an untrained person involved. At least she's powerful, so she won't be a liability.

"That is a tight timetable. I appreciate the heads' up, and your help so far. We'll get it done. I'll let you know, even though I'm sure Brynn is keeping an eye on the situation," I pause, checking my notifications. "I just got your email. Thanks again, man."

"It's no problem. Let us know if you need anything else. We'd come along as back up if we could, but you know Brynn wouldn't like that." A moment later, he disconnected.

I walk back over to the guys, who are deep in conversation about something. They stop talking as soon as I get close enough to hear them. "We have Jericho's location and schedule; and less than twelve hours to get it taken care of before Will and his team are sent to handle us."

Opening the email from my friend, I pull up all the intel he sent and show it to my team. We'll have to clue Zola in on our plan, but that can wait until we formulate it. "Will said he's heavily guarded and these schematics show a crazy security system. I'm not sure how long it will take us to get through it," I admit, pointing out what I'm talking about.

"It sounds like we don't have a choice, so let's get a plan together. With this schedule, it's not likely that we'll be able to sneak in with a crowd and gain access. We're gonna have to take another approach," Griff says.

"But what will work?" Brady asks. "We can't just go knock on the door and tell him we're there to kill him."

GRIFFIN

"Why can't we?" I stare at my friends for a moment before explaining myself. "Not the *'Hey, we're here to kill you,'* part. But the knock on the door and ask for a meeting. He's a cocky, self-important, businessman after all. There has to be a way to get a meeting with him. Once we're in the building or his office, we take him and his security out. Then we're done. Easy peasy."

Brady and Nico stare at me for a moment. "Have you lost your fucking mind?" Brady snarls. Nico just shakes his head in disbelief.

"Think about it," I say, pacing as I talk. "We go ask for a meeting, make it look like we're smugglers or suppliers or something. He's gotta have connections if he's this high up on

Brynn's list. That means he has people who sell to him and buy from him. We just need to be one or the other, right?"

Brady stares at me in disbelief. Nico holds up a hand. "He might be right. It could work. But we need more information. What is Jericho buying and selling? What does he need? I'll check the reports Will sent and see if there's anything helpful there."

"Do you think she'll be okay with this?" Brady asks me.

I ponder for a minute before answering. "I don't know. With the way she defended herself against the break-in, I think she can handle it. I can't say if it will hurt her emotionally to be part of ending this man's life, though. It's not like we can leave her here alone while we go deal with Jericho."

He nods. "I know. I just don't want to cause her any harm. We may not be able to keep her out of this, but we can keep her hands clean. I know it won't be easy, but we have to try."

I could argue with him, since I know Zola's secret, but it's not my place to tell him about her dark side. Who knows? Maybe she's already told him, and that's why he's feeling extra protective. The only way to find out is to ask her, and I'm not sure I want to know about their pillow talk. It's bad enough that he gets to sleep with her and we don't. I can't handle knowing the details of that arrangement.

"You should probably apologize for tackling me anyway," I offer, giving him a reason to seek her out. "Then you could explain the situation and find out how she feels about it."

He nods and walks away. I stare after him for a while before realizing that I don't have time to consider my relationship or lack thereof with Zola. We need to prepare for this job.

BRADY

I don't apologize. Ever. For anything. So, why am I rushing down the hall, looking for Zola so I can tell her that I shouldn't have attacked my friend? I should tell her that she needs to accept what the bond makes me do. It's not my fault I'm jealous and overprotective. That's a lie that even I won't believe. But here I am, hunting her down to apologize for overreacting and tackling Griff when he got a little close with an attack.

What is wrong with me? This mating bond is worse than I expected. I should have tried harder to avoid putting myself in a situation that I know is going to end badly. But here I am, chained to my fated mate and fighting against the pull of it while drowning in the emotions that bond created. Fuck my life.

Using the bond to track her, I find Zola in my room. That shouldn't surprise me, since she's basically moved in with me. The bond makes it difficult for us to spend much time apart, even if neither of us is outwardly excited about it. And while I am going to apologize to her, it won't be for attacking Griff. It'll be for not trusting her to protect herself, and maybe for not giving her a chance to connect with the other guys.

I push the door open, sputtering and choking as I'm assaulted with a spray of water. "Bad kitty!" Zola scolds, glaring at me. I narrow my eyes at her, stalking forward as if I'm hunting her. Forgiving the attack will be easy, but her comment is what lights my blood on fire. My alter ego doesn't like being called 'kitty' at all.

My shift comes on quickly and without any encouragement from me. One moment, I'm stomping across the room to tackle my mate to the bed, the next, my clothes are shredding, bones are breaking and rearranging until my human form becomes an oversized snow leopard. It happens so fast that I barely recognize the pain.

Standing over my mate, teeth bared, I realize that I can't communicate with her in this form. So much for apologizing and smoothing things over. Instead, I'm sure snarling at her is going to make things so much worse.

"You came to apologize?" she asks, her eyes going wide, as if she'd heard my thoughts.

That can't be, can it? It's not possible for mates to share thoughts. Someone in the pack would have told me about that when they explained mating bonds, right?

"I don't know how it's possible, but I can hear you in my mind." She shrugs. *Does it work in reverse?* Her voice dances in my head, and it's my turn for shock.

I don't understand how this is happening. I send the thought to her as easily as if we were having a conversation.

Neither do I, but it is kinda neat. At least now I'll have some insight into that caveman brain of yours. If I wasn't a snow leopard right now, I probably would laugh. Instead, I chuff at her and nuzzle my head against her torso. If she minds being pinned to the bed by a huge predator, she doesn't show it. Part of me wonders if she's that brave or if she trusts me that much.

I have my answer when she reaches out and wraps her arms around my head while dropping a kiss between my eyes. *I trust you. I know you won't hurt me.*

And just like that, I have control of my body again, easily shifting back to my human form. Curious, I send one more thought toward my mate, wondering if our bond will allow silent communication in this form as well.

"Absolutely not! I won't accept your apology unless it is spoken out loud, and in detail," she insists. "I want you to tell me exactly what you're sorry for, and admit what you did wrong." Well, at least I know we can communicate without everyone knowing what we're discussing.

I growl at her playfully, then press a kiss to her lips, my naked form pressing hers to the bed. Rolling my eyes, I give her what she wants. "I am sorry. I won't apologize for jumping Griff, though. I will admit that I was wrong to not trust your ability to defend yourself."

She eyes me thoughtfully for a moment. "Accepted."

When she wraps her arms around my neck and pulls me down for another kiss, I lift myself so I'm hovering over her. "And I'm sorry I haven't stepped back and given you a chance to decide if you want to bond with Nico and Griff. I'm fighting against the jealousy in the bond, but sometimes, it wins. I'll try to do better. Just keep calling me on it when it happens."

I lower myself for the kiss she wants, letting everything go except the feeling of her lips on mine and our bodies pressed together.

For a moment, being mated isn't as horrible as I'd expected. I'm still worried about what will happen when she's in danger and I have a job to complete, but we'll deal with that when it comes up, I guess. And if she bonds with the other two soon, I should have less to worry about, since I know that they'll protect their mate as thoroughly as I will. If I'm honest, I know they'll protect her now, but that doesn't help the bond loosen its grip on me.

When I finally break the kiss, I roll off her to lie on my side. "Oh, no. I don't like that face you're making. What's wrong?" she asks, reaching over to trace my brow with her fingertips.

"We found Jericho, and have to move on him within the next few hours. If we can't take him out, we become the next targets. And we can't leave you here while we take care of it. You have to come with us, so we can make sure you're safe," I explain.

"So, what do we need to do to get ready? How can I help?" she asks.

"You understand what I mean when I say 'take him out', right?" I ask for clarification. I don't want her thinking she's okay with this, then freaking out when we have to kill this man.

"Brady, I know what you guys do for a living. I may not fully get the why of it, but you have to kill this guy or the Fae person will send a bunch of assassins after you. I get it. Griff says that the guy is bad, so I don't object. Tell me how to help," she answers.

ZOLA

The look on Brady's face is priceless when I tell him that I know we have to kill Jericho. I may not understand why they have this job, but it's important that we get it done. If for no other reason than saving our own lives.

I'd love to say that I don't enjoy killing, but that would be a lie. It's a thrill like no other, especially when I know that the person I'm offing has hurt people and deserves the retribution I'm delivering.

And honestly, I've been missing the rush of it since we've been hiding. Training is fun, learning to fight against different types of attacks and figure out my opponent's weakness. But it's not the same thrill as hunting down a target and feeling their life drain from their body; knowing I'm the one in control—that their suffering is up to me.

"We should get with the guys and work out a plan of attack. Are you sure you're okay with this? Taking a man's life isn't easy," Brady says, and his concern is touching.

"I know. After this is taken care of, we should talk about my past. I'm not nearly as innocent as you think. But there's not time to go into all of that right now. We need to get Jericho taken care of so we can figure out this whole fated mate thing and get our family settled," I say, pressing a quick kiss to his cheek and climbing from the bed.

His eyes go wide, but I'm not sure if it's curiosity or lust causing it. I don't know how he or Nico will react to my secret. Griff understood, and didn't judge me for my actions. I can't be sure that the other two will feel the same way. All I can do is hope that my past isn't a deal breaker for this. I want these men more than I've ever wanted anything before.

I won't give them up now. But could they have a double standard when it comes to killing? It would destroy me to learn that they disapprove of my past actions, or my desire to continue. And it's not like I'm a serial killer. I'm a vigilante, seeking justice for those who can't pursue it on their own.

At least that's what I tell myself, even if the truth is a little darker, and a lot more hidden.

JERICHO

NICO

WHILE BRADY GOES OFF to apologize to Zola and explain our situation, I pull out my laptop and go over the files Will sent me. As I read through everything, I realize a couple of things. Number one, Will's girl is an impressive hacker. Number two, Jericho is more of a threat than we'd originally thought. If we don't take him out this time, he'll definitely be onto us, and we'll be running from him and the guild.

Documents detailing payments received for 'goods and services' make up dozens of pages in the records. I dig as deep as I can, hoping to figure out what exactly that means, but can't find anything tangible. He appears to deal in power, but I'm not sure how he's obtaining it, or transferring it.

"These records don't make sense," I mutter, scrolling through more pages.

"We don't have time to figure it all out," Brady says, strolling into the room with Zola behind him. "Is there anything that will help us get to him?"

"Maybe," Griff pipes up from across the room. "It looks like he's buying and selling people with powers. Or he found a way to drain or transfer their power to someone else, I'm not really sure of the details."

"That's what I've been trying to figure out, too," I admit.

"So," Zola says, pausing for a moment, "you need to approach him as if you have someone powerful to sell, and get to him that way."

"I think so, but I don't know how to convince him that we have something he wants," Griff says.

I lock eyes with Zola and shake my head before she can answer him. "No."

"What do you mean, 'no'?" Brady asks.

"We're not 'selling' you to Jericho. Even if we're right there with you the whole time, and we know you're safe, it's not happening."

She crosses her arms over her chest and glares at me. "It's the only way you're going to get close enough to him to finish the job. Besides, it's not like I can't take care of myself. I might even be able to take him out for you."

Her confidence may be more bravado than anything, but I have to admit, she's powerful. Possibly enough so that Jericho would want her.

"I don't like the idea, but she's right. With what she's been able to do during training these past few weeks, we may be able to convince Jericho that he needs her," Brady offers. And just like that, I want to punch him in the face. How could he want to use our mate that way? Especially when he's the only one who's bonded with her.

Griff steps forward and takes Zola's hand. "Are you sure you can handle this? It's not like what you've done before."

What is he talking about? I can't help wondering exactly what she's done in the past that would make him that concerned about sending her to do this but wouldn't make him object to it.

"I know, but I can do it. I'm stronger than I look. Besides, how else will I prove to you three that you don't have to be so overprotective?" she smirks.

With Griff and Brady completely on her side, I know that I have no chance of changing her mind. But I have to try. "Dewdrop, could I speak to you privately while the guys get things ready?" I hate giving in, but clearly, I won't win this one.

She nods, and the guys leave us alone to talk. "I know what you're going to say," she offers.

"How can you, when I'm not sure myself?" I counter.

Zola steps closer to me, wrapping her arms around me. "I know you're worried that I'll be hurt. I promise, Nico, I'll be fine. You can send some shadows with me if that will make you feel better. But I'm pretty powerful on my own."

Raising on her toes, she presses her lips to mine, and sparks light behind my eyelids as they flutter closed. I groan and deepen the kiss, pulling her harder against me. My hand fists in her long, dark hair as my tongue strokes along hers. She sighs and relaxes in my arms.

A strange sensation dances along my skin, like goosebumps and static electricity mixing together. My body warms and my shadows surround us. I've never felt anything like this before.

ZOLA

The moment Nico deepens our kiss; I feel the mate bond snap into place. It's a strange sensation, but I realize that I've felt it before. When I bonded with Brady, I was so caught up in my orgasm that I didn't recognize the electric zap that indicated our connection. Hopefully, the bond will help him to trust me, instead of making him feel more protective.

Are you going to fight me on this idea, or let me prove myself? I try to project the thought to him as I pull away from our kiss, watching his face to see if this works the same with him as with Brady.

"What the fuck? Did you just talk to me in my head?" Nico's eyes go wide and he gapes at me.

I smirk at him. "Welcome to our mate bond."

"I, but, how?" he sputters. I can't stop my laughter. "What's so funny?" he asks.

"I have no idea how it happened. I'm just sure that's what that electric feeling was, and now we can communicate in our heads. It's amusing that I recognized it but you didn't, since you and Griff wanted to explain everything to me," I say, still laughing.

He grins at me, finally accepting what I've said. My heart warms as I feel his emotions join Brady's in my soul. There's still one piece missing, but I can't assume bonding with Griff will be this easy. We don't have time today to find out, either. Once this is finished, I'll make it a point to claim Griff, too, and then we can figure out how we're going to make this work. For now, Jericho has to be the priority.

GRIFFIN

As much as I don't want to use Zola as bait, I understand why she thinks it's the best idea. One look at Brady, and I know he feels the same. So, we'll give her a chance to convince Nico. Even if he doesn't concede, it's three to one, so we know what's gonna happen.

Besides, he doesn't have to like it to let her prove to herself and us that she can handle it. I don't think she's shared with Nico or Brady about her past yet, and I won't be the one to tell them. It can wait until she's ready.

I follow the instructions Will sent to get their help one last time. With his girl's tech abilities, she can easily set up a meeting between Jericho and us to "sell" Zola. Fifteen minutes after I hit send, Will responds with a time and location.

"The meeting is set," I tell Brady, just as Nico and Zola return from their conversation. I relay the information to everyone, making sure that we're all on board with the plan. Nico simply nods, looking annoyed. "So, she convinced you?"

"Not exactly," Zola answers before he has a chance.

Brady and Nico exchange a glance. "Seriously? You weren't gone long enough—" my shifter friend says.

"Apparently our bond was closer to complete than yours. Perhaps a lack of resistance on my part made things easier?" Nico answers.

Fuck me. Nico and Zola bonded in the few minutes we left them alone. I can't say being the odd man out feels good, but there's no time to dwell on that right now. "Well, we have a job to do, and not much time left to get it done. So, we should focus. We have to meet Jericho in two hours, and it's gonna take an hour to get there."

Changing the subject doesn't make me feel any better, but it does distract me. I show them the map and explain where we're meeting Jericho and, I assume, his men. Because what kind of trafficker shows up to a deal alone?

With everything laid out and gone over half a dozen times to make sure we aren't missing anything, we get our supplies together and head out. I can't portal us to the location, because that would give away my power level. It might also destroy our cover story, if Jericho or his men noticed us portaling from the gala when Nico and I had to go help Zola.

The drive across the city takes longer than I anticipated it would because of traffic. "We still have plenty of time. Stop freaking out," Brady orders from the driver's seat of his SUV.

"This is insane. I should have just portaled us there," I say, knowing it wouldn't have been a good idea, even if we could have made it early.

Nico shakes his head. "Not possible. Just take a few breaths and let Brady drive. He'll get us there in plenty of time."

Zola chuckles from her spot next to Nico. "I have an idea if you guys trust me."

Brady looks at her in the mirror and nods. Nico and I both say, "Do it," at the same time.

Her chuckle turns into a dark laugh as she closes her eyes for a second, and lightning strikes the stop light. Somehow, it only takes out the ones parallel to us, and the ones in front of us turn green. Traffic starts flowing quickly, as if people know this is a mistake and it'll all stop soon.

"How did you do that?" I ask in awe.

"I used lightning to short out the light system, twisting it a bit to make the ones we need green and the rest red. I have no idea how long it will take the city to fix it, but we should be able to get where we need to before they can replace the fried chips," she answers easily.

I'm constantly amazed by this woman. If I'm honest with myself, I'd admit that I'm already falling in love with her, even though we've shared two brief kisses and she's bonded to my two best friends. I'm not going to deny it, but I'm also not going to advertise it. My feelings are an issue that can be addressed after we finish this job.

Closing my eyes, I focus on breathing; meditating to center myself for what's coming next. My eyes fly open when the SUV comes to a stop. "What's wrong?"

"We're here," Brady says. We should have fifteen more minutes of driving, but it seems Zola's trick with the lights has helped us arrive early.

"We all know the plan. Since Brady and I can communicate with Zola silently, we'll know that she's okay even if Jericho has his men take her away from us. She's going to note every detail of everything between where we start and where she ends up. Hopefully, he keeps her with us during negotiations," Nico says.

"I'm gonna have to demonstrate my power, right?" she asks.

"Most likely," Brady answers. Zola nods as if she expected that response.

"Do you have something in mind?" I ask, considering what she could do to prove herself powerful enough for Jericho to want her.

"I figure taking out at least one of his guards should prove how much I'm worth, shouldn't it?" she smirks.

"As long as he thinks we have you under control, that is an excellent idea. We don't want him to think you're a danger to him, though," Brady says.

"So, I can't completely kill one, but I can get close?" she asks.

Brady and Nico nod in agreement. "That should work," I say. As much as I don't want to do this, we climb out of the SUV and head to the meeting spot.

ZOLA

I let Nico bind my hands behind my back and follow Brady toward the meeting spot. My heart races at the idea that I'm basically trapping myself to help them kill a man. Reminding myself that this particular man is way worse than any of the ones I've already killed doesn't seem to help my nerves. My stomach twists, and swallowing becomes difficult. I gulp down air, letting the panic take me.

Are you okay? Brady's voice sounds like music in my head.

Freaking out a little, but I figure that will help make this look real. My response is sincere and blunt. There's no point in lying to him when he can see through it into my emotions.

"This will be over soon," he says quietly. I know he's right, but a sudden feeling of despair washes over me. I hope this ends the way we want it to. Maybe Nico was right about this being a bad idea.

You've got this, dewdrop. And just like that, my confidence bolsters a little. We walk around a corner, and see a man in a suit with four guys standing around him. This must be Jericho. A shiver runs down my spine, and I wonder why he seems so familiar.

"Ah, it's nice to see you've arrived a bit early. It's so frustrating to deal with people who waste my time by showing up late," the man says, brushing invisible lint from his sleeve. He gives off an air of superiority and indifference at the same time.

"We're anxious to get this deal over with. Debts to pay and all that," Brady says in response. As we step closer, I feel Nico's shadows weave through my fingers. That small gesture of support means more to me than he could realize. My nerves are threatening the whole job, and I have to get them under control.

"Yes, I was told that you have something very powerful for me today," Jericho says.

Brady nods, and Nico gives me a gentle shove forward. Griff steps to the side to let me through. I stop short just out of reach of the tall, wiry man, my eyes lock on him as I try to figure out why he looks so familiar. Where have I seen him before?

"Your pet doesn't need to be part of our negotiations, but I will need a demonstration," he says, dismissing me from his presence.

"Do you have anything particular in mind?" Nico asks, looking from me to Jericho and back. It would be so easy to steal the breath from him, to pull the liquid from his body, to sprout vines from the ground beneath his feet and wrap him in them.

That got dark fast, Kotik.

Are you okay, dewdrop?

Their concern is touching and startling. I need to keep a better handle on my thoughts, especially since they don't know my secrets yet. *I'm fine. Just thinking about ways I could help move this along faster so we can go home.*

They clearly appreciate that idea, and I'm nearly overwhelmed with warm, caring thoughts through the bond. I get distracted and miss part of what Jericho says. I shake my head to refocus my thoughts. *What did he say?*

"Do I need to spell it out for you?" Jericho says, his voice tinged with annoyance.

He wants you to take out one of his men. Your choice. Brady says in my head. Well, that's convenient. The man we're here to kill wants me to demonstrate on one of his guards. Either he doesn't like them, or he isn't convinced I have enough power.

With my eyes locked on Jericho and my hands still bound behind my back, I focus my thoughts and power on the guard standing nearest him on his right. Within moments, the man is clawing at his throat while his face turns blue. When he drops to the ground, I release him for a moment.

"Finish it," Jericho orders. So, I do. As soon as the guard is dead, Jericho claps. "Fantastic!" He motions for his remaining guards to take me away, but Griff steps closer to me.

"We won't let you take her until our negotiations are finished," he says, wrapping a hand around my arm. "I'm happy to give you a few minutes with my friends in private to come to an agreement."

Jericho scowls, but nods. His men follow Griff as he leads me a few yards away. We can barely hear what's going on, but I trust Nico and Brady to keep me updated.

Less than five minutes later, Jericho motions for us to return. "You drive a hard bargain, gentlemen, but I think we've come to an amenable agreement."

When Brady nods, I wrap my power around Jericho's three remaining guards, choking the life from them while Nico's shadows envelop Jericho to hold him still. Once the guards are dispatched, Nico's shadows unbind my hands.

"What the hell?" Jericho cries, looking from one of us to another.

"It's nothing personal," Griff says. "This is just business. Surely you understand that."

Before Jericho can respond, I notice that Brady has stripped down to his boxers. His snow leopard rips through his skin and pounces on the target. I watch in awe as huge jaws clamp down on the neck of the man who wanted to buy me, tearing out his throat. Crimson covers Brady's white coat, shining brightly in the dim light.

Arousal builds inside of me, and I try to outweigh that feeling with disgust at the fact that watching my mate kill someone is getting me wet. Brady drops Jericho's body and turns to me, cat eyes wide with desire. My eyes meet Nico's and I see that he's feeling the same burning need I am.

Not giving us a moment to act on the lust that we're drowning in, Griff throws me over his shoulder, opens a portal and darts through it.

My Decision

GRIFFIN

With the amount of lust washing over everyone, it's clear that if I don't act fast, this massacre will turn into an orgy. Since I'm not fully certain that's what Zola would want, I grab her and portal back to our hideout. The job is done, and the guys need to bring Brady's SUV back anyway.

Once we're in my room, I walk to the bathroom with Zola still on my shoulder. "What the fuck are you doing, Griff?" she asks, slapping my back as I carry her.

"You three were about to do something that you might have regretted later when you aren't under the influence of their emotions, Elskede. I'm simply saving you from that," I answer, lowering her to the floor in front of me after I close the bathroom door.

"So, you decided the best way to stop a sex party was to take me to your bathroom?" she smirks. I shake my head and turn my back to start the shower.

"Yes, I did. Because I'm not going to let either of them get to you until everyone has calmed down. Mate bonds are volatile at times, and people make rash decisions by acting on someone else's emotions. It's more intense when there are multiple partners. I've seen this before, and it didn't end well," I explain.

She pauses, as if my words finally start to sink in. "You're serious."

"I am. I've seen a man killed by another of his fated mates' lovers during a situation a lot like the one you almost got into back there. I'd rather not have to try and break something like that up, and I'd rather not bury any more friends because someone's hormones got out of control."

"I thought you were jealous and wanted me to yourself," she says, all humor gone from her voice.

"As much as that's true, that wasn't the reason I took you away from them. I would never stand in the way of your mate bonds, unless your safety was at stake. I understand if you're upset with me, but I feel this was the best thing for everyone.

I'll be outside when you're done showering. There are extra clothes in this cabinet if you want something clean to wear after you wash up," I explain, showing her where I keep some shirts and shorts.

I know the bottoms won't fit her, but at least she can cover herself with one of my shirts. I'd love to say that my only concern right now is her modesty, but honestly, I'm dying to see her in my clothes. I would never force my mate bond on her, especially with the stress and excitement we just left behind.

ZOLA

After Griff leaves the bathroom, I strip down and get into the shower. I've been using Brady's shampoo for so long that I nearly forgot that other scents exist. I let myself get lost in the citrus and woodsy scent I associate with Griff as I scrub my body and hair.

Stepping out of the shower blade wrapping one of Griff's thick towels around me, something pink on the counter catches my eye. Did my warlock leave me a note? That seems weird, but these guys do like to surprise me.

I dry my body, pull on one of Griff's shirts and my underwear, then wrap a smaller towel around my hair. Taking a deep breath, I finally grab the hot pink cardstock and turn it over.

Zola,

You have been selected for an opportunity to audition to join the Cursed Blade.

If recruited, you will be provided targets that align with your moral compass. You will be given access to unlimited funding and equipment. You will also have the opportunity to recruit your own team, or join the one you've been assisting.

If interested, be at the docks in exactly twenty-four hours. This is a one-time opportunity, and will not be offered again.

We appreciate your discretion in this matter.

We hope to see you soon.

~ B

What the hell is this? The Cursed Blade. Why does that sound familiar? Wait. My heart races as the thought crosses my mind. I rush out of the bathroom with the note in my hand. The moment my eyes lock with Griff's, I know exactly what this is.

The look of terror in his eyes is all the confirmation I need. "I don't really have a choice, do I?" I ask, shoving the paper at him.

"You do," he insists. "But refusing would mean giving up your mate bonds."

I nod, wondering if that was even something I could do. I know it's not, no matter how tempting the thought is. Running away isn't the answer. Even if they asked me to, I wouldn't. I can't walk away from my mates, even if I haven't claimed them all yet.

"Can you tell me what to expect?" I ask, sitting next to him on the bed.

"I wish I could. Every audition is different. All I can say is be prepared for your greatest fears to attack you. Fight as if your life is on the line, because it is. If you fail the audition, you won't live," he explains. Fuck. This is more intense than I expected.

"Well, I have twenty-four hours to prepare. What do you suggest?"

Griff pulls me into his arms and holds me tightly against his chest. Fear grips my heart, and for a single heartbeat, I consider what he's told me. I could run, but I'd be giving up my future. If I fail, I'll be giving up my life. Am I prepared for that? I don't know. How can a person be prepared for this kind of situation?

I won't give up, though. My happiness is within my grasp for the first time in my life. I refuse to let it go without a fight. If the Cursed Blade wants me, they're gonna get me.

The door flies open, Brady and Nico stomping inside. At least they've taken a minute to clean up first. I'd imagined them storming in, still covered in blood.

"What the fuck were you thinking?" Brady starts on Griff. Before my warlock can answer, Brady notices the paper. "What is that?" His face pales, and he takes a tentative step toward us.

"She's been invited," Griff answers, handing the note to Brady. Nico pulls me from Griff's arms, engulfing me in a hug that includes his shadows.

"We can't let this happen," Nico swears.

"We're not going to," Brady vows.

I shake my head, pushing Nico back. "This isn't your choice to make. It's my invitation, and it's my decision. I'm not giving you guys up just because you're scared, I can't handle the audition."

Both men blink at me, as if I've grown an extra head. "I don't think you understand," Brady starts. I hold up a hand to stop him.

"I understand. I'll be facing my worst fears, and if I survive, I'll be a part of this guild until my death. If I don't survive, you three will do something stupid, like attacking the guild and getting yourselves killed too. So, I guess you'd better hope I survive."

My announcement shuts them all up, and I walk back to Griff's bathroom. I take my time brushing my hair and giving them a chance to process what's happening. They discuss the situation as if I'm not even a part of it.

"We can't let her do this," Brady insists.

"I don't think we can stop her," Griff argues.

"Then we need to convince her that she shouldn't do it," Nico counters.

"You do realize that I can hear you, right? And that talking about me as if I'm not right here pisses me off. This isn't up to you; it's *my* decision. And I've made it. I am going to this audition, with or without you. It'll be a lot easier with you, but I'm sure I can find my way out of here if I have to."

I refuse to back down or give in to their desires. I won't abandon my fated mates because I'm scared of what's coming. With that decision made, I stroll out of Griff's room and make my way back to Brady's, since that's where all my things are. I dress quickly, weave my hair into a braid, and head to the training arena. Whether they're going to help me or not, I have to prepare. Facing this challenge isn't going to be easy, and I need to make sure I'm ready.

I wish that they could see my point; that they would support my decision. But I guess that's too much to ask for. So, I'll do this on my own. Then maybe they'll trust me to know my own limits. I just hope I'm not making a huge mistake and giving myself more credit than I actually deserve.

When I get to the training arena, I start with the stretches and yoga poses Griff taught me to calm my mind. I'm learning that it helps with concentration and mental strength. When

I finish those, I move to the weightlifting area Brady has been teaching me in. I'm careful not to overdo it, but I feel physically stronger when I work my body this way.

As much as I want a break, I push through. Stopping only to catch my breath and get a drink of water, I work through my weight routine. I stretch again to cool down, then wrap my hands and move to the sparring section. This is where Nico and I focus on anticipating what someone will throw at me.

I've done some sparring with all three guys, and my fights with Nico usually incorporate magic along with physical attacks. Just when I start to think I'm ready, a shadow wraps around my foot, and I'm lying face down on the floor.

"I thought you were ready for anything, dewdrop," he says with a smirk.

"And I thought you objected to me accepting this audition," I counter, rolling over and jumping to my feet.

"Yeah, I still kinda do, but something tells me I don't get to make this decision for you," he answers.

"Hmm. And just how did you come to that conclusion?" I ask, wrapping my arms around his neck and raising on my toes for a kiss. His lips press to mine for a brief moment, then he pulls away.

"To be honest, it was Griff. I think the fact that you're not bonded yet makes him the most level headed of us. He's convinced that you can do this, simply because you want to. After we talked, he went to find Brady and make him understand too," Nico explains.

I don't know how to respond. I wouldn't have expected the man who told me to run away to be the one convincing everyone else that I'm capable of handling this. Tears fill my eyes, and I wipe them away quickly.

"So, are we gonna practice, or have you changed your mind?" he asks, raising an eyebrow at me.

I take a step back and blast him with water in response. His shadows wrap around me again, trying to knock me over. I push them away with a strong wind, then dart toward Nico. The element of surprise is my friend, and I know I can overwhelm him if I move fast enough.

I jump to tackle him, but shadows wrap around my body, catching me in mid-air. "It seems you've been caught, dewdrop. Now what?" he asks, smirking.

I fight against the shadows while trying to think of a smarter way to get out of his hold. A bright enough light would banish the shadows, at least long enough for me to get free and reassess the situation. Flames appear in my hands, growing more intense until the shadows finally dissolve.

NICO

The brightness of the flames makes me wince more than the heat of them. It's enough to make me drop hold of my shadows and squeeze my eyes shut. I know she's powerful, but none of us have seen this from her yet.

Zola slams against me, knocking me flat on my back. Air rushes from my lungs, and it's impossible to tell if it's from the fall or if she's using her magic to prevent my breathing. My eyes fly open and lock with hers. The look on her face tells me everything I need to know. She's holding my air hostage until I submit.

As much as I don't want to give in, I have to. If I don't, she'll kill me. Admitting she's got me pinned isn't easy for me, but I tap the ground three times. With a satisfied smirk, the air rushes back into my lungs. "You could have killed me," I pant, not angry, just trying to make a point.

"And they'll do worse than that to me at the audition if I let my guard down," she counters. It's a fair point, and I'm glad she understands how serious accepting this is.

"Don't let them get in your head. No hesitation, no mercy. You can do this; I'm sure of it," I admit, hating that the only way I get to keep my mate is if she survives this trial by combat. Part of me wants to take her and run away, but I know that's not practical. If it was, Brady would have already done it. I hope Griff is having some luck getting him to understand that this is the only way. We don't have to like it; we just have to stand back and let it happen.

BRADY

"I don't think you get it, Griff," I say, repeating myself—again. "I physically can't stand the idea of letting her do this. It's like ripping my heart out and asking me to keep moving."

My friend looks at me for a moment. "I do understand, though. And while our bond isn't complete, I feel it too. I don't want her to do this, but she refuses to give us up. If that's her choice, we have to help her prepare."

"She refuses to give us up? Why would she have to?" Clearly, I'm missing something here. Griff is more insistent than usual, and there has to be a reason.

"If she refuses the audition, she won't be able to stay with us, given that we're part of the guild. Brynn would never allow it. And Zola knows that. So, she's decided that her only chance to be with her fated mates is to accept the audition, and fight. For us," he says.

Well, now I feel like an ass. My mate decided to join us so she didn't lose us. And Griff is right; Brynn probably wouldn't let her stay with us if she refuses this offer. "You make a good point. We need to help her get ready. She has to ace the trial or it won't matter what we want. Do you really think she's strong enough?" I hate myself for asking, but even with us living together, I feel like Griff and Nico know her better than I do.

"I know she can do it. As long as she has our support. So, let's go get our girl ready to defeat Brynn's torture," he says, walking toward the door.

I focus on Zola through our bond and realize that she's with Nico in the training arena. "It looks like Nico got on board faster than I did, huh?" He gives me a look in response and we make our way to the arena.

The moment we open the door; I feel Nico's tension and pride through the bond. It's weird that I can feel his emotions as well as hers, but I don't question it. "Oh, good, you're here. Our girl needs more of a challenge," Nico says, panting as he tries to hold her still with his shadows.

I look from him to her and back, wondering what we've missed. Without waiting for a response, Zola throws a stream of water at me, and a blast of air at Griff. My warlock friend easily blocks the attack, redirecting the air to force the water to hit me harder. Fucker.

Rolling out of the way, I debate shifting. There's no way to know what Brynn will throw at Zola, and we need to get her ready for everything. But will she expect me to shift? I need to catch her off guard. I decide to stay in my human form a while longer, making sure to block my thoughts from my mate, so she can't use the bond to anticipate my movements.

It doesn't seem to matter when she sends vines to wrap around my legs at the same time she sprays me with water again. I go down in a tangle of vines and my own legs, growling as my snow leopard fights to the surface. I'm still not ready to shift, so I drop and feign defeat, giving myself a minute to watch her and figure out the best way to attack.

A wall of fire traps Nico in the corner, blocking his shadows from reaching her. I'm amazed that she can keep that going while trapping me with vines, and still using her air and water powers to go after Griff. Sweat beads on her brow, and I can tell that Zola is getting tired. If I wait a little longer, I should be able to overpower her and pin her down.

Hesitation tugs at me. I don't want to make her think she can't do this; I just want her to understand that she can't underestimate any enemies at any time. I realize that it's not helping anyone if I don't put my all into this. While she's distracted, I shift, crawling out of the vines to creep behind her and pounce.

Surprises

NICO

After Zola's training session, we make her take a nap. She's bound and determined to do her audition today because she doesn't want to wait until the last minute. With a little persuasion, Griff convinces her to lay down for a bit. Because our bond is so new, she insists I join her while Brady and Griff prepare for what's coming.

I hold her as she sleeps, letting my shadows wrap around us while I rest. We stay that way until Brady tugs on the bond to let us know it's time to get ready. As much as we want her to avoid this, it's better for everyone if Zola accepts the audition as soon as possible.

Once everyone is dressed and ready to go, Griff portals us to the docks where we know Brynn will be waiting. Walking into the warehouse brings back memories of my own audition, where I met Griff and Brady. It was a free-for-all fight between twenty people, and the winner would get the job. Brynn's intention was to hire one person, and bury the rest. The whole thing took three days, and by the end of the first day, the three of us were a team.

Part of me wonders if this fight will be like that, or if Brynn has something completely different in mind for our girl. Since her invitation said she could join us, I'm guessing they won't be pairing her up with anyone else. Brynn is hard to predict though, so we have no way to know what's coming.

GRIFFIN

The moment we step inside the arena, the doors disappear behind us. Typical Brynn. There's only one way out of this. Let's hope Brynn doesn't make us go through the audition against Zola, because I'm not ready to die today, and I won't kill my mate. I think there's actually something in Fae law forbidding pitting mates against each other, but I'm not certain.

My power flexes under my skin as we walk to the edge of the arena. If Brady is right, we'll be escorted to the top level to watch while Zola battles whatever monsters Brynn created or recruited for this. I don't like it, but I won't stand in my mate's way. This is the only way she can stay with us, and we all know it.

Besides, if what Nico told us about his friend Will's team is true, the guys were pretty soft when they auditioned to become part of their girl's group. The three of them were allowed to work together, but she had to watch and hope for the best. I'm pretty sure that's what we're about to endure, and that idea terrifies me. I don't want our girl going in there alone. Sadly, it's not my decision to make.

BRADY

Brynn poofs into existence, and I instinctively step in front of Zola. I know it won't stop what's coming, but in the moment, I can't stop myself.

"Hello, gentlemen. I see you've brought my latest candidate to me. Does that mean that you'll be joining me in the audience to observe her skills?" Brynn's voice drips with disdain, as if they'd expected us to drop Zola off and go home to wait for the results.

"Brynn. I wish I could say it's a pleasure, but it's not. I'm sure the guys agree with me; this is not what we pictured for our mate. But—she's decided it's what she wants, so we're here to support her in any way we can," I answer.

The Fae's pink eyebrows rise in shock. Apparently, not everyone can see a mate bond when a connected pair or pairs enter a room. That's good to know.

"Your mate? Oh, dear. That could complicate things. I certainly hope she can prove herself, so you boys aren't destroyed by her death," they say with a smirk. Turning to Zola, Brynn continues, "Are you prepared to face the darkness inside of you, little witch?"

ZOLA

I'm not sure what I expected, but Brynn certainly is not it. Hot pink hair, pale pink skin that glimmers in the light, and a lithe body that makes it nearly impossible to tell if Brynn is male or female. Even their voice is confusing, sounding a bit like two voices working together in harmony. Not that it matters who is planning to torture me today; I'm not backing down.

"I'm as prepared as I can be, since I have no idea what's going to happen," I answer with my chin lifted. Honestly, I'm terrified of what I'm about to be thrust into. My mind races with different scenarios, each one worse than the last.

"She'll be fighting on her own, right? No groups this time," Nico says. I can feel his nerves through the bond, and realize that I may not be as alone as we'd all thought during this fight.

"Of course, the little witch will be battling solo. I can't promise that she'll only have one foe to deal with at a time, but that is entirely up to her and how she goes about the maze. Sadly, I'm not able to predict how long this audition will take, so we'd best get things started," Brynn says, waving their hands in a flourish.

Without any further warning, I find myself standing in front of a stone wall with an opening twice as big as Brady's SUV. Fear freezes me in place, and I stare at the opening.

"Come, now, little witch. You must reach the center of the maze, defeating anything that attacks you, by any means necessary. Be sure you're using any and every skill you have; you're going to need them. And don't worry about holding back your powers—that won't help you here. Time to begin," Brynn's voice echoes above me, and I look up to see if I can find where they're watching from.

We're up here with Brynn, Dewdrop. A tendril of shadow creeps from a recessed window, and I know where my mates are. I take a deep breath, then step into the maze. The first few feet are easy enough. The beginning of the maze is filled with spiders and bugs that are no match for my control of flames. I head down a corridor, turning away from the charred bodies of insects.

A few feet further, I run into a shifter, but something is wrong with him. It's almost as if he's feral, or rabid. I don't let him get close, trapping the wolf in a bubble of air and compressing it. I should be squeamish about killing, but I've been warned that everything here is out to get me. Closing my eyes for a moment, I silently ask for forgiveness, then snap the wolf's neck.

The maze continues this way for a while, small beasts and challenges I have to defeat or overcome to keep going. At one point, I come to a solid wall. *Do I blast through it, or go back?* I point the thought toward Brady, wanting to make sure I don't do something that could be considered cheating. When he doesn't respond, I take a moment to consider the exact wording of Brynn's instructions. *By any means necessary.*

That gives me a defense if Brynn decides that they don't like my methods. I raise my hands to the wall and use my earth powers to crumble it with an earthquake. As the stones crack and fall, I look up to the recessed window where I know my mates are watching. Pausing for a minute, I wait to see if Brynn will object to what I've done. When no such objection happens, I walk through the opening, instantly regretting my actions.

On the other side of the wall is a giant scorpion. Fuck my life. Why did I think I could handle this? I should have just run when I had the chance. It's too late for that now. All I can do is fight for my life. If I don't survive, my mates will have to find a way to live without me.

Steeling myself against the racing of my heart, I bend and twist my magic into a shield of air and a sword of fire. If I can attack before the scorpion does, I may have an advantage. For half a second, I think it hasn't seen me yet. One more step forward proves that I'm mistaken about that. This enormous fucker turns and looks at me, stinger poised and ready.

Its first strike hits my shield, barely stopping before the stinger would have gone through my head. I focus on growing vines through the dirt floor, wrapping them around the scorpion's legs and tail to hold it still. While shooting water at its face, I slowly move around its side and ram my fire sword into the beast's side, slicing through its armor.

I push more fire into it, tearing the scorpion in half. With the tail severed, I can focus on the head and pincers. I wrap a bubble of water around it, condensing and squeezing, until the front half of the scorpion pops inside the bubble.

Covered in sweat and gore from the monster I've just killed, I look up again, wondering if my mates have a better view of me than I do of them. I know I can't afford to get distracted now, since this fight is getting more intense every path I take. I'm starting to worry about what's waiting for me at the end of this mess.

Shaking my head to clear my thoughts, I take a breath to center myself, the way Griff and Nico taught me. Since we can't communicate now, I'm guessing that Brynn is blocking our bond somehow. I wonder for a moment how the guys reacted to that.

Picturing Brady's face when he realizes he can't tell me what to do makes me laugh. I scrub my hand down my face as I walk down another path. One more turn, and I'm standing in a square. Is this the center? Did I make it? Somehow, I think this was too easy, even though that scorpion nearly killed me. Joining this guild can't be this easy, can it?

I don't have time to consider those questions, though, because darkness surrounds me and two spotlights come on over strange circles on the ground. The hair on the back of my neck stands up, and a shiver goes down my arms. If I didn't know better, I would think lightning was about to strike. That thought doesn't scare me. I've been able to deflect lightning strikes since my fifth birthday.

Armed with my own confidence in my powers, I stare at the pillars of light. What does Brynn have for me now?

"Good job, little witch. You've made it to the center. But since you skipped several of the challenges I had set up for you, I have something extra special for you to take care of," Brynn's voice echoes from above. "You're aware that you've been hunted since your birth, I'm sure. It's time for you to see exactly who is responsible for that. Here's your chance for revenge."

A man with dark, shoulder-length hair steps out of the shadows. No, it can't be. It's not possible. "Raj?" my voice breaks, and I can't move as the man steps closer.

"Zola, I had hoped it wouldn't come to this. Unfortunately, we couldn't control you long enough to finish our job," he answers in a raspy voice that doesn't sound like the man I remember.

I turn my head as movement to my left catches my attention. I'm not as shocked this time, because if Raj is alive, that means Amara must be too. She steps out of the shadows into the spotlight, confirming my suspicions.

"The two of you are responsible for my parents' deaths? I thought you were their friends," I spit. This does explain why I wasn't taught much about my family or tribe. If I was actually stolen by traitors for some nefarious purpose, why would they want me to know how powerful I really am?

"Oh, child. We only ever did what we had to in order to protect ourselves. And if it makes you feel any better, Raj was against the idea at first. Then when he saw how wealthy and powerful it could make us, he changed his mind. But it wasn't easy for me to convince him," Amara says. Her voice is honeyed and softer than usual.

Conflicting emotions overwhelm me, and I drop to my knees. "How could you? You betrayed your best friends for wealth and power. That's insane. They loved you like family," I insist, even though everything I know about my parents is what little these people told me.

"It's sweet that you believe everything we told you. For a time, we were friends with them. But there are things you don't know about us; things that will change how you feel about trusting us. With good reason, but things could have been very different if your tribe hadn't tried to exile us," Amara says.

"Was anything you told me true?" I can't stop the question, even though I know I won't trust the answer.

"We never lied about wanting what was best for you," Raj insists.

"And what exactly did you decide was best for me?" I ask, fighting against the tears that are trying to fall.

"Taking you to Jericho so he could give us your power, of course," Amara laughs.

"You were working with Jericho?" Relief washes over me, knowing that my mates and I already handled him. He can't hurt me now, and neither will these two parasites.

"We've been informed of what's become of him, and your part in it. While I'm not thrilled to lose such a useful ally, I am relieved that we will no longer have to pay for his services. We'll just have to find a way to transfer the power ourselves," Amara answers.

I knew this audition was going to be difficult, but I never imagined I'd have to fight against the very people who raised me. I thought of them as family. Guilt ate at me after their deaths, which I'm guessing were faked. "Why fake your deaths?"

"It was all part of the plan," Raj answers.

"We needed to disappear if we were going to take your powers. It's not like you'll survive the transfer, and we didn't need people asking questions about where our daughter went. I guess we could have made it look as if you'd run away, but this way, we're free of that damned city. Once we have your powers, we can go back to the village and take over," Amara explains.

I shake my head, trying to process her words. It makes no sense and perfect sense at the same time. I could never understand why they wouldn't tell me about my parents or village.

But I guess isolating someone makes it easier to mold them to your will.

"Stealing my powers isn't going to be easy. I'm not just going to give them to you. You'll have to kill me first," I insist, drawing a fire ball out of the air.

"Oh, child. We need you alive for now. You'll die soon enough, don't worry. And it will only hurt a lot. So, if you want to extend your suffering, that's fine. We can fight; but you're going to lose," she laughs again.

Suddenly I'm aware that she's been trying to distract me so Raj can get behind me. It's a decent tactic, but also one that Brady has taught me to counter. I say a silent prayer of thanks for my mates and how well they've taken care of me, then something hits me.

"Why would you ask Brady, Nico, and Griff to take care of me if anything happened to you? That's the part that makes no sense. If your plan is to kill me and take my powers, why recruit protectors?"

Amara glares at me. "What are you talking about, child? We never did that. Who are those people?"

"If you didn't do it, then who did? They told me it was you," I insist.

"Clearly, they're delusional. I never asked anyone to take care of you. Did you, Raj?" She turns her attention to her mate.

He looks as confused as she does. "No, love, I didn't. I have no idea who those people are, either."

A laugh echoes in my ears, and I wonder why Brynn would be so amused at this conversation. "Well, someone pretended to be you and asked these guys to take care of me if anything happened to you. As a result, I'm not as weak and helpless as you expect me to be."

I don't have time to ponder who's responsible for my current situation or why; I'm just thankful that someone cared enough to send my mates to find me when I needed them.

"We'll just see about that," Amara snarls. "Remember, Raj, we need her alive. She's no good to us if she dies."

Her words put things in perspective for me. They need me alive, otherwise, they'd just kill me. And Amara already said that the power transfer will kill me. So, these people who cared for me and raised me never actually cared for me at all. It was all an act.

Hurt stabs through me, sadness for what I lost by not knowing my parents, sadness for my parents being duped by these assholes, and pain for the time I spent mourning my caretakers when I'd thought they were dead.

I let the anger course through me, harnessing its potency to bolster my resolve. Just because they aren't going to kill me right now, that doesn't mean I need to go easy on them. With my pain and rage to guide me, I let the darkness take control. I will be the one walking out of here, not them.

Audition Complete

ZOLA

With my emotions in overdrive, it's hard to remember what the guys taught me. I know that I need to calm down, but there's no time. Instead, I embrace the darkness as it swallows me whole. Once I stop fighting it, I feel my full power coursing through me. I've never felt anything like it. This isn't the pull of the elements; there's something else inside me, and I'm not sure what to do with it.

My vision goes black, then everything changes. I blink a few times to clear my eyes, and I can see everything in a weird heat vision-like state. This will definitely make attacking people I thought I knew a little easier. I throw back my head and scream, a high-pitched, terrifying sound that cracks the glass of the viewing window above.

With fire in both hands, I turn to the first multi-colored blob and release both blasts at it. I'm not sure if it's Raj or Amara, and I find that I really don't care. The flames take hold, immersing the figure as they scream. When I turn back to the other figure, they're gone. I guess I'll have to hunt them down.

One glance over my shoulder tells me that the one I set on fire has crumpled to the ground. When the flames start dying down, I push my power at them, forcing the fire to come to life again. I know better than to think I've won, but this will at least slow them down.

A floral scent hits my nose, and I know that Raj is the one on fire. Amara's favorite perfume gives her away, leading me in the direction she ran. I walk slowly, making sure to watch my back in case Raj figures out how to extinguish my flames.

As I track Amara, I send random gusts of air toward where I left Raj, encouraging the flames to keep growing. Searching left and right, I'm starting to wonder how she's hiding from me. I shake off the darkness, blinking as it recedes.

"Hello, darling," Amara says, standing right in front of me. Her fist slams into my face, and I fall backward. Fuck, that hurt. How did she shield herself from my power?

I don't have time to worry about that; I need to make sure I take her out before she knocks me unconscious. I pull vines from the ground and start wrapping them around her legs to hold her in place. Warmth creeps up my back, and I turn to see Raj stumbling toward us, flames still clinging to his skin.

Before I can hit him with another burst of fire or blast of air to stoke the flames, Amara douses him with water. His charred skin smolders and he screams in pain. I send my vines up her arms to stop her from casting magic. I hit Amara with a brick made from air; satisfied when she collapses on the ground.

Then I turn back to Raj. He's still coming at me, even though his skin is burnt off in places, and barely hangs on in others. I have no idea how he's still standing with as much pain as he must be in. Vines climb his legs, wrapping around his arms.

"Zola, it doesn't have to be this way," he rasps. "We can escape now; just you and me. I never wanted to go along with Amara's plans. You know you're like a daughter to me."

His words freeze me in place. All I ever wanted was a family to love me, to want me, to protect me. I thought I had that with Raj and Amara. But it was all lies. Just like now. He's still lying.

But what if he's not? Can I really kill a man when I'm not completely certain he's as evil as his mate? That thought stops me for another moment.

"Zola, please. You have to believe me. We can be a family, just like before. You and me," he says, his eyes going wide at something behind me.

"Thanks for the warning, Raj," I say, forcing my vines to pull his arms apart until he screams. I twirl around to face Amara, the smirk on her face making me think that Raj was just trying to distract me so she could get free.

I duck when she sends a blast of water at me. "You know what I don't understand?" I ask as I put up a shield of air and push her back with it. "How do your powers keep changing?"

Amara laughs. "You're far too trusting, Zola. You assume that everyone is like you. We never were. That's what got us exiled in the first place. We're power leeches. We can take power from others. Not on the scale we need to take what you have, but it's enough to let us do what we need to."

Hmm, power leeches. The thought sends a shudder through my body. How disgusting! I start to ask how that works, then decide that if it's anything like regular leeches, I don't want to know.

"Well, that's gross," I say, pushing another wave of air at her to shove her a few feet further from me. As soon as I let the air drop, she blasts me with a stream of cold water, sending a layer of ice over me to freeze me in place.

Fire erupts from my skin, and I feel the darkness creeping in again. This time, I won't let Raj interrupt us, and I won't let Amara hide from me. I'm exhausted—physically and emotionally, and I want this done.

I point one hand at Amara and the other at Raj. Flames engulf Raj again as a spear made from vines flies into Amara's chest. Pushing the flames to burn hotter, I thrust the spear of vines through her back, encouraging them to spread out as they move, tearing her into pieces.

"I told you, I'm not as weak as you think," I growl as her life leaves her eyes. Once they're glassy and empty, I set the corpse on fire to ensure that she can't come back from this.

Then I turn to Raj again, a smile spreading across my face when I see that he's nothing but a pile of ash now. I stand there, watching Amara burn, until there's nothing left of her, too. A moment later, as ash swirls in the air, the reality of what I've just done hits me.

These people raised me, and I killed them. For real this time. I didn't get them hunted down; I murdered them. *How am I supposed to feel about this?* The thought crosses my mind, and I barely register the arms wrapping around me and pulling me into the hard chest.

You're allowed to feel however you feel, dewdrop. Nico's voice in my head is calming, even though I'm numb.

"Congratulations, little witch! You are now a full-fledged member of the Cursed Blade Assassin's Guild. The benefits are many, and your mates can explain everything to you once you've recovered from today. I know this wasn't easy, but you had to be the one to do it. None of us could deal with this situation for you. I, for one, am glad to see that my minor interference didn't change the ending Violet saw for you," Brynn says with a huge smile.

BRADY

Holding Zola to my chest, I glare at Brynn. "You could have told us what was going on. We could have prepared her better. What if they had killed her? Or knocked her out and portaled away?"

"My darling boy, that would not have happened. As I said, Violet predicted this outcome. I had no doubt that your little witch would survive this encounter. Now, please take her and go. I'll be in touch when I have a job for you," Brynn waves a hand to dismiss us.

Zola stares at the wall, completely unaware of anything that's happening around her. "She's in shock. We need to get her home, cleaned up, and let her rest," Nico says. I nod in response, scooping Zola into my arms while Griff makes a portal to take us home.

Since Jericho is handled, we go back to our main hideout, even though it may be triggering for our girl since she actually killed someone there, too. It doesn't matter, because we're not going to be here any longer than we need to for her to recover. Once she's back to herself, we'll find a new place where we can start over as a family.

I take my mate to my room, strip her out of her ruined clothes, and climb into the shower with her. I focus on washing her tenderly, keeping things as non-sexual as I can. There will be plenty of time for fucking later; right now, she needs to be clean and rest. Once she's clean, I dry her off, tug one of my t-shirts over her head, and tuck her into bed.

Then I nudge Nico through the bond, getting him to bring Griff. "Is she okay?" Nico asks, pushing my door open without knocking.

"More or less. I think we should talk about sleeping arrangements. Since she's mated to all three of us, I think we need to conjure a bigger bed and all start staying together," I suggest.

"Shouldn't we wait for her to recover to make sure that's what she wants?" Griff asks.

Nico shakes his head. "I agree with Brady. This way we can take turns caring for her, and not have to move her too much. And she'll feel way safer with all of us here. She'll never be alone, unless she asks to be."

Relief washes over me at how easily Nico speaks my thoughts. I couldn't get the words right to explain what I wanted to do for her. Maybe that's why our girl has three mates; one of us couldn't take care of her the way she needs.

"We'll work as a team; just like when we're on a job, but better, because we're taking care of our mate," I agree, realizing that I sound like a lovesick fool. And maybe that's not the worst thing that could happen to me, after all.

Griff nods, then turns toward the bed. "You'll need to move her, so I don't accidentally hurt her with the magic."

Nico grabs Zola, cradling her in his arms and stepping behind Griff when he starts casting. We don't usually get to see him create things with his magic, so this is a new experience. We're so used to destroying things; it's a nice change to be nurturing something for a change.

Sweat beads on his brow as Griff works to expand my mattress to fit the four of us. Magic swirls around the bed, making it disappear in a cloud of blue twinkling light. The light gets brighter until I have to close my eyes against it.

When the light fades away, I open my eyes to find Griff on his knees, panting. Nico has shadows wrapped around himself and Zola. In front of my warlock friend is a magnificent bed that looks big enough for six people instead of just four.

"That's beautiful," I breathe.

"Good job, Griff," Nico says. "Are you okay?"

Griff nods. "I just need to rest now, like our girl."

Nico lays Zola on the bed, and I tuck blankets around her while the guys go and get what they need from their rooms. We can worry about everything else tomorrow, or whenever our girl feels better.

I press a kiss to her forehead and lay down beside her. "We're here with you, Kotik."

ZOLA

Once I realize that Amara and Raj are dead, I feel numb. I expected relief, or sadness. Instead, I got a sense of nothingness that kept me from responding to Brynn, or reacting to anything my mates say or do after they take me home.

I'm vaguely aware of Brady suggesting that we all stay together, but darkness pulls me under before I understand what he's talking about.

I wake feeling more myself, but still drained. My power feels depleted, and I crave the sunshine. With their job done, and my audition complete, not to mention the people who wanted to steal my power dead, I guess it might be okay for us to come out of hiding.

"Elskede, you look like hell," Griff says, pulling me into his arms.

"Thanks, that's just what every girl wants to hear after she kills her adoptive parents," I tease. He tenses, his arms still around me. "It's okay, Griff. *I'm* not okay yet, but I will be."

I turn my head and press a kiss to his lips. With a little bit of persuasion on my part, by tugging on his hair, I get him to deepen the kiss as I roll on top of him. Pinning him to the bed, I grind my core on his growing erection before letting him break the kiss.

"I don't think that's a good idea. Not until you're fully recovered," he insists.

"And who decides when that is?" I ask, crossing my arms in a pout.

"Someone besides the girl who completed her audition then went into shock," he answers with a smirk. "Besides, I want our first time to be something we'll both enjoy, Elskede."

"I'm fine, and if you don't want me, I'm sure one of the other guys does," I pout.

Griff looks at me as if he's judging how serious I am. "Okay. If you can conjure all four elements at once and hold them for five seconds, I'll let you have your way. If not, you have to do what I say today," he says.

His suggestion makes me want to balk, but he can't possibly know how weak I'm feeling, can he? Determination in my eyes, I nod. "Fine." Raising my hand, I will fire to spark. Then in my other hand, I grow a small flower. I use my air power to rustle the flower and stoke the flames. But when I try to summon my water, I lose hold of all my magic. The flower disappears, the flames die out, and the wind vanishes.

Gritting my teeth, I try again. Nothing. Not even a tiny spark. My magic is gone. I've never felt like this before, and I don't know how to deal with it. Clearly, Griff knows something I don't, because he smirks at me.

"You used too much during your fight. It's going to take time to refill your stores," he insists. "And since you have to listen to me for the rest of the day, we're going on a picnic to help you recover."

I start to object, to complain that a picnic isn't going to help me recover. Then I realize that it sounds like a relaxing way to spend the day. So, I nod, then climb out of bed and head to the shower.

"What happened to the bed? This is Brady's room, right?" I ask when I realize how much bigger the bed is than it should be.

"We made some adjustments while you were asleep," Nico says, walking through the door. "Do you like it?"

"It's huge. Like big enough for the four of us," I say, realizing, "Wait. You guys agreed to play nice? I don't have to split my time between you?" My eyes go wide with delight. I'd been wondering how being mated to all three of them was going to work.

"No, Kotik, you don't have to split your time or choose who you're going to be with. But we are all going to have some say in what happens as a group. No one will be forced into anything that makes them uncomfortable," Brady insists.

I turn to face him, realizing that he just came out of the bathroom. The sight of him in a pair of jeans, shirtless, scrubbing a towel over his hair makes my mouth dry.

"I don't want anyone to be uncomfortable," I mutter, staring at his naked chest, still glistening with drops of water.

"Good," he says, stepping forward to press a kiss to my nose before walking to his closet to pull out a shirt. It's a damn shame to cover up that chiseled perfection. As I have the thought, I sway on my feet and realize that maybe I'm not ready for group fun just yet after all.

Nico catches me before I can fall, easing me back to the bed. "You really should be resting. I know Griff wants to get you outside for a while to recharge your power, but that can wait an hour or so while you sleep a little more and get something to eat."

As much as I want to argue, I can't. "Can I take a bath instead of sleeping? Or sleep then take a bath before the picnic?" Even as I ask, my eyes feel heavy and I don't know if I'll be able to stay awake long enough to get the answer to what I've just asked.

Nico and Griff tuck me into the bed, fluffing pillows behind me and making sure I'm warm enough with soft blankets. It's almost like being in a cozy nest.

Brady crawls into bed with me. "You can take a nice, long, hot soak after you wake up. There's no rush. You need to rest so you can recover. We can discuss everything in detail when you feel better. For now, at least one of us is going to stay with you at all times."

I hum in satisfaction as my eyes flutter closed.

FINALLY

ZOLA

I STARTLE AWAKE, MY heart racing. I know that I've been in and out of consciousness for a while, but I'm not sure how long it's been. The sun feels good on my face, and I take a deep breath in. Wait, I should not be able to feel the sun from here. Where am I?

My eyes fly open, then close at the brightness. When I open them again, shielding with my hand, I can't see. Temporarily blind, I try to reach for my powers to determine my surroundings. I vaguely remember the empty hollow feeling in my chest when I tried to use my powers to convince Griff I was okay. That feeling is gone, and I feel all four elements nearby.

A few minutes go by with me just soaking in the feeling of nature around me with my eyes closed. Then I push my magic out a little further and a shiver runs down my spine. My guys aren't here. I'm alone, clearly not in the city. I sit up slowly, blinking until my eyes adjust to the brightness.

Brady? Nico? Griff? Where are you? I can feel the bond, but I know they're not here.

You're okay, Dewdrop. Griff is nearby. Brady is taking care of some business, and I'll be back with lunch in a bit. Nico's voice is comforting in my head. But if he's right, and Griff is nearby, why can't I sense him?

Oh, shit. I haven't completed the bond with Griff! I push myself up to my knees and look around. Nico didn't tell me where I am, but he said I'm okay. He wouldn't say that if this wasn't a safe place. My breath hitches as I take in my surroundings. This is the most beautiful, natural space I've ever seen.

Standing up slowly, I turn in a slow circle, feeling the breeze on my skin. My bare feet wiggle in the grass, enjoying the cool feel of the dirt. The warmth of the sun shining on me brings a smile to my face. I need to find Griff. I don't want him to think that he's not important to me.

"Griff?" I call as I start to walk toward the trees that surround this clearing. I sense the stream before I hear it, and hear it before I get close enough to see it. But when I finally get close enough to see the clear body of water, my mouth goes dry.

Griff steps out of the water, dripping, in nothing but his boxer briefs. At that moment, I want nothing more than to lick the water from his skin, drying him with my tongue. His eyes lock on mine, and I'm certain that he knows exactly what I'm thinking.

"Elskede! You're awake," he exclaims, his eyes going wide, as if he's shocked to see me walking.

"I feel like I've slept forever," I respond.

He laughs, "It's been a week since you tried to seduce me. You have no idea how hard it was to resist you that night. And even harder to convince the guys that you needed to be in nature to recover. I can't wait to rub it in that I was right."

"A week?" I ask. "I've been unconscious for a week?"

"You used nearly all of your magic in the audition, and nature magic isn't exactly easy to replenish when you're locked away underground," he explains. "You didn't show any improvement until yesterday, when I finally convinced them to let me bring you here."

I throw my arms around him and press a kiss to his lips. "Thank you." I kiss him again and his arms pull me closer. "Where are we?"

"My family's homeland. We're safe here. You have nothing to worry about," he insists, hugging me tightly to his chest. "There's a portal in the house that's enchanted to only let the four of us through it. The guys will be back later."

The warmth of the sun and the dampness of Griff's body collide against my skin, making me shiver. "I'm so sorry! Let's get you inside to dry off," he says, pushing me away from his nearly naked body.

I shake my head. "I'm fine, really. It feels good, and it's warm enough out here. I won't get frostbite." He doesn't laugh at my joke, and I decide to try another tactic. "I can think of other ways to warm up, though, if you're that worried about it."

My eyes wander up and down his body, taking in every inch of exposed skin. I'm barely controlling myself right now; I want him so badly. My power crackles through me. I didn't realize how much I missed it after the audition, but I did spend most of that time unconscious.

"If you're sure you're feeling better...I'm going to need a demonstration to prove it," he counters.

I twist my hand, tossing a fireball into the air and catching it with a gentle breeze. Carefully, I bring it down to eye level and make a flower grow from the center of the flames. Griff's eyes go wide, then I splash some water on it, and the whole thing disappears. "Is that a good enough demonstration?" I ask, trailing my hands up his chest to link them behind his head.

His lips capture mine as he drags me back to press against him again. He deepens the kiss and the whole world seems to vanish. My eyes flutter open to find four walls surrounding us, one made entirely of glass. In the center of the room, right beside us, is a plush round bed piled with pillows. Griff kisses me again before scooping me up and tossing me onto the bed.

I squeal at the suddenness of it, laughing as he crawls up my body to capture my lips again. "I've been dying to get you in here, Elskede." Griff presses kisses to my cheeks and down my jaw to my neck. "You are absolutely perfect. I can't believe I get to be part of your life."

His words, along with his lips, send shivers down my spine. I slide my hands up his arms to his shoulders. Digging my fingers into his hair, I fight the elastic tying it into a bun until his blonde waves tumble free. He groans as I scrape my nails along his scalp.

My mind races, but I can't form words. Instead, I let all the little sounds go, moaning or sighing when Griff kisses me, whimpering when his hands skate along my skin. Desperation grips me as he slowly removes my clothes. "I need more," I breathe against his mouth as he ghosts his lips against mine.

"Patience, Elskede. I'll take care of you," he whispers. His hand moves down my body, fingertips barely touching my skin. My nipples pebble at the feather-light sensation. I expect him to stop his exploration there, but he keeps moving, down, down, down, until his fingers dance over my center. Without warning, he dips a finger inside of me, withdrawing it and popping it into his mouth. "Mmm, delicious," he says as he drags his tongue along the soaked digit.

Eyes locked on mine, he returns his hand to my apex, continuing the gentle touches that are driving me crazy. My body feels like I'm on the verge of combusting, and if I don't get some relief soon, I'll go up in flames for sure. Griff teases his fingers along my clit, flicking and stroking, as he moves them to trace my opening.

I lift my hips, trying to guide him to exactly where I want to be touched, but he moves with me, keeping his touch light and just shy of what I want. "Stop teasing me," I demand.

He laughs and continues his slow ministrations, drawing out every sensation. If I want things to move faster, I'm going to have to lead. Reaching for his waistband, I drag his boxer briefs down and wrap my hand around his cock. His groan sounds like a combination of pleasure and torture, and I smirk. I love knowing I have this kind of power over him. I move my hand up and down, lazily stroking him.

"Oh, yes," he mutters, thrusting into my fist harder.

Knowing I'm on the verge of getting what I want makes me giddy. I squeeze him again, then release him to drag my fingers along his throbbing dick. Making his breath hitch bolsters me again. I want him, and I want him now. No more waiting.

I push him onto his back and climb on top, rubbing my soaked pussy along his erection. The first waves of an orgasm grip me at the contact. I barely manage to stay focused enough to guide him to my opening and slide down on him.

The burn of him stretching me is delicious, and I move slow to drag it out. Lifting myself up, I come almost all the way off him, then slide back down even slower than before. Griff stares at me, watching every move I make, his hands gripping my hips and trying to move me faster. Instead of cooperating, I gyrate my hips, rolling them in small circles as I slide down. His groans of pleasure and frustration push me over the edge, and as I start to fall into my climax, Griff flips us over and pins me to the bed.

"My turn. I hope you're ready for fast and rough. I don't think I can hold back anymore," he growls. I drag my nails down his back in response, pulling him toward me so our lips can meet again. As he kisses me, devours me, possesses me, he pounds into me. Griff's thrusts get harder and faster, going deeper every time until I scream his name, giving myself over to the sensations he brings to life in me.

My orgasm triggers his, and he bucks against me as he comes, his eyes locked with mine as he cries out my name. We stay locked together for a long while, breathing hard, trying to catch our breath.

That was intense. Brady's voice echoes in my head. Griff winces. Shit. I hadn't even noticed the mate bond snapping into place. I planned to shield him from the other guys at first but got too distracted. "I'm sorry. I completely forgot that they'd be able to tell when our bond was complete," I offer, pushing away from Griff.

"It's fine. I wasn't prepared for commentary from someone who isn't involved, was all," he laughs. We climb from the bed, and he leads me to the bathroom. Once we're cleaned up, we head back through the house, with Griff showing me each room until we make it to the kitchen.

NICO

Knowing that Griff got to fuck our girl before me, even though my bond with her was formed first should be annoying, but it isn't. I know I'll get my turn soon and having the four of us bonded feels amazing. I hadn't even known there was something missing until the bond snapped into place.

Now I feel whole, and I understand why I was drawn to these guys during our audition for the guild. We were all meant to find each other. This is my family.

When Zola and Griff enter the kitchen, Brady is stirring the chili, so I cross the room first to scoop her into my arms and kiss her. I'm gentle until she deepens the kiss, darting her tongue along mine. Then, I hug her to me tightly and kiss her harder. I twirl her around, pressing her against the wall with my entire body. Zola grips my shoulders, hopping up to wrap her legs around my waist.

I know I can't have her right now; she needs to rest. But it's so hard to resist the urge to fuck her on the counter right now.

I'm not sure Brady or Griff could handle that right now. Her melodic voice in my head startles me for a second, and I realize I wasn't exactly keeping my thoughts to myself.

Sorry, Dewdrop. I wasn't trying to pressure you. I don't want her to feel obligated to sleep with me just because she's been with my friends and we're all bonded to her.

Zola captures my lips with hers again, devouring any thoughts I had. She grinds her core against me and my dick strains against my shorts at the heat of her. "Perhaps the two of you would like to take this out of the kitchen?" Brady growls. "I'm trying to make lunch here, and you're very distracting."

I break the kiss long enough to look over my shoulder at him, then lock eyes with our girl. Cocking an eyebrow in question, I smirk at her. Zola laughs and nods, wrapping her arms tighter around my neck. I give Brady and Griff a salute as I carry her out of the kitchen.

We start kissing again and she claws at my back. Using my shadows to navigate, I carry her to an empty room close enough to the kitchen for there to be no doubt what we're doing. Glancing around, I notice we're in the den. "Couch or desk?" I ask, nipping at her jaw.

"Desk," she pants. I could just sweep everything off the desk onto the floor, but my shadows make that unnecessary. They quickly clear the space enough for me to set Zola on the edge of the desk. I release her long enough to drag my shirt over my head and toss it on the floor.

The moment I step back, she strips out of her shirt and leggings. My cock throbs when I notice she's not wearing anything underneath. "You are gonna be the death of me, but what a way to go," I breathe, dropping my shorts and stepping between her legs.

"I have no idea what you're talking about," she says, smirking. Her fingers wrap around my hard length, guiding me to her entrance. I groan when she slides my cock through her folds, spreading her wetness around.

ZOLA

Nico finally gets the hint and thrusts into me, sliding me further onto the desk before he realizes and drags me closer by my hips. His mouth crashes against mine as our bodies come together at a feverish pace.

I love the idea that I can make him feral for me. Nico trails kisses across my jaw, licks his way down my neck, then sinks his teeth into the top of my breast. An orgasm tears through me at the sensation of his canines marking me.

The scent of his desire mixed with mine is intoxicating. Every sensation adds to the next until I'm reduced to a mass of overstimulated nerve endings. My pleasure borders on pain, and I love it. Rough sex had never been my thing before, but I revel in the way Nico owns my body.

He braces one hand on the desk behind my ass, locking me in place. Then he snakes the other hand between us where his fingers find that needy spot at my apex that's begging for his attention. When his fingers brush against my clit, another orgasm tears through me. My release builds as he pinches that little nub between his fingers and rolls it back and forth.

"Nico, I can't. It's too much," I pant against his shoulder.

"Yes, you can. You're taking me so well, Dewdrop. Let go and ride the pleasure," he orders. I cry out as his fingers keep tweaking my clit. He slams his cock into me, rocking the whole desk.

Feeling overwhelmed by everything he's doing to me, I bite down on his shoulder to stifle my screams. I can feel his desire growing, as if knowing that he's destroying me gets him off.

His pride at knowing that Brady and Griff can sense what we're feeling should annoy me, but it doesn't.

Seeing Nico take control like this is hot, even if I feel like I'm dying from his methods. He strokes my clit again, thrusting his dick into me harder. The desk gives way, its leg cracking from the force of Nico's pace. For a moment, I think I'm going to hit the floor, but instead, shadows wrap around us, holding me in place while he grabs my hips and pounds into me even harder.

I wonder if this is what a sex swing is like, then remember that all three of them can hear my thoughts. The chuckles I get in response through the bond confirm that we have no secrets here. I feel my face heat, and I bury it in Nico's chest.

"It's okay, Dewdrop. Your curiosities are nothing to be ashamed of. If you want to see how similar it is, we can get a swing and test it out," he says, not even winded from how fast and hard he's fucking me.

Lifting my head to meet his eyes, I expect to see amusement, but the only thing there besides desire is love. He's completely sincere about exploring my 'curiosities' as he calls it. The idea of that leads my mind down a rabbit hole of kinky thoughts, ramping up to my next orgasm. This time, I take Nico with me, plunging us both over the edge into bliss.

He kisses me gently, easing out of me as his shadows lower me to my feet. Nico's arms wrap around me, and I can tell he's not ready to share me with the guys yet. There's no animosity about it, no jealousy, no desire to keep me all to himself...other than for a few more minutes.

I feel nothing but love and support through the bond with Griff and Brady. I love how they each understand that having

a few moments for just the two of us, no matter which two it
is, is important.

Epilogue

THREE YEARS LATER

ZOLA

I HESITATE FOR A moment before pulling the door open and walking into the warehouse. Being summoned by Brynn is not a usual part of being a guild member, and I'm honestly a little nervous. The fact that the summons said to come alone makes it worse. I have no idea what to expect. All I know is that Brynn is Fae, and no one knows the extent of their powers.

"Fantastic, Zola, you're right on time," Brynn says, appearing out of thin air as soon as the door closes behind me.

"Shit, Brynn! You scared me," I answer.

"Apologies. I'm certain this situation is nerve wracking for you. I can assure you that no one here means to harm you in any way. This is a necessary encounter, though. I have much to tell you," the Fae says, gesturing for me to follow them down a hallway.

What the actual fuck is going on here? I get an immediate summons to meet Brynn, and it's just for a talk? Confusion doesn't even begin to explain my emotions right now. We stop in front of a door, Brynn opens it, and motions me inside. As much as I want to refuse, I want—no I need—answers.

The room is cozy, with a couch and three chairs circling a fireplace with a low flame going. "Please, take your coat off and get comfortable. I'll have refreshments brought in, then we'll talk." Brynn closes the door, leaving me alone.

I dig my phone out of my pocket and remove my jacket. Sitting in one of the chairs by the fire, I send a text to the group chat, letting the guys know that I'm okay. I know that they followed me here, and they're camped right outside to make sure I'm safe.

The door opens and Brynn strolls back inside, followed by a wheeled cart with refreshments on it. Magic is strange, but I'm learning to recognize other people's powers more all the time. The cart stops in front of me as the door clicks closed. Brynn takes a seat on the couch across from me.

"What is this all about?" I ask, wishing I'd sounded more annoyed than curious.

"I am aware that you've been searching for answers to a few pressing questions, my dear. I have found myself in possession of some of those answers and would like to provide you with the information I have," they answer.

"I'm listening," I say, refusing to react. I'm not sure what questions they're referring to; I've been asking so many since I discovered my guardians were not what they seemed.

"First, let's review your questions. Then I'll tell you what I know," they offer. I nod, and they continue, "Very well. Question one — why are you being hunted? Question two — who is after your power? Question three — will you ever be safe?"

I take a cup of cocoa when Brynn offers it, blowing on the hot liquid before sipping thoughtfully. I see we've decided to start with the biggest questions. Taking another sip, I enjoy the rich chocolate while I wait for Brynn to explain.

"Well, from what I've been able to discover, you were being hunted because of your power. It appears that you have some extraordinary abilities, the likes of which others in your village have never seen before. In addition to controlling each of the four elements, something about the combination gives you power over storms, too," They pause, examining my face for a long moment.

"You spoke to members of my village?" I ask.

They nod, "Sadly I am not able to introduce you. I wasn't even able to meet with them in person. They've all gone into hiding because of Amara and Raj's betrayals and will not come forward. But I did get more information about your powers and controlling them. I will send the files to one of your gentlemen."

"That does explain why I seem to be special to whoever it is," I answer.

"That brings us to our next point. Who is after you?" Brynn asks with a smirk. I sit up a little straighter, my eyes widening. "I'm afraid I have some good and bad news on that front. Amara wanted your powers, that's true. However, my sources indicate that Jericho was going to double cross her and take your powers to sell to the highest bidder. They aren't the only ones who were after you for your abilities, though."

I stare at Brynn. "Do you know who else was hunting me?"

Their smirk grows. Of course they know. Somehow, they seem to know everything. "My darling, that is the bad news." They pause, no doubt for dramatic effect, while running long fingers through their pink waves. "It appears as if *I* am the other party who was hunting you. I wasn't aware of who or what I was seeking, but I did have some feelers out that would track your magic. And the moment I realized you were with Brady and his crew; I tried to send you an invitation."

"That first pink orb that Griff said was there to kill us. That was intended to deliver an invitation, wasn't it?" I know I'm right before Brynn even reacts. A laugh bubbles out of me. "Amusingly enough, I don't think I have any reason to be afraid of you. Yes, you want to use my power, but you don't want to take it or kill me. Thank you for helping the guys rescue me."

"My darling child, you saved yourself. You ran when danger presented itself, yes, but you didn't run far or for long. A plan was formulated, and you faced your fears. I'm so proud of what you've become. It took real courage to face your former guardians and defeat them. My only regrets are that I cannot reconnect you with your tribe."

A knock sounds at the door, and a short, magenta haired woman walks in without waiting for Brynn to answer. "I'm sorry to interrupt, but Zola needs to get back to her mates. If she doesn't leave now, they will storm the compound, and it will end badly for everyone."

"Ah, Violet. Thank you for that message," Brynn says, dismissing her. "Violet is my psychic. She has many abilities that are outside a normal psychic's range, similar to your witch powers. I'm sure that she's seen a flash of the future, so I will let you get back to your men. I'll be in touch soon."

And just like that, I find myself standing outside in front of Brady's SUV. I stomp over to the driver's side door, stopping three feet away from it, and prop my hands on my hips. "Seriously? After everything we've been through, you guys can't let me have a private meeting with Brynn?"

Brady looks annoyed, Griff has the decency to dip his head in shame, but Nico just grins at me, as if he's proud of himself. What am I gonna do with these guys?

"It's not that we don't trust you. We don't trust Brynn," Nico says.

"So, you thought you'd storm the compound and start a fight no one could possibly win?" I chide.

"Wait, how did you know what we were considering? We made sure to keep our thoughts shielded from you," Brady says.

"Violet saw it all go down, and apparently, felt the need to stop it before you got yourselves killed," I sigh, rolling my eyes at them. I love these men, but they are reckless sometimes.

"Let's just go home," Griff suggests.

I nod, climbing into the back seat with Nico. For me, home is anywhere these three are.

"Home sounds perfect."

A feeling of satisfaction washes over me as we drive back to our house outside of the city. It's not as private as Griff's family home abroad, but it's ours, and I have access to nature. Knowing that I'm finally free relaxes me in a way that shouldn't be possible considering what we still do for a living. I smile to myself as I watch the tree line of our property come into view.

Home.

Acknowledgments

I would like to thank:

My author besties, who encourage me to keep writing, even when it's hard;

My amazing PA, Gwen, who is my twinsie;

My Alpha Team who tries hard to keep me on track;

My Editing Team who does their best to make sure my books make sense and have as few typos as possible;

My Cover Artist (Wallflower Designs) who's responsible for the gorgeous images on the front of this book

and My ARC Team, who catch some of the things the rest of us miss.

About the Author

M.P. Starkweather is a wife, mother, author, poet, casual online gamer, self-proclaimed fan-girl, and full-time nerd. She writes free-form poetry, paranormal romance, sci-fi romance, reverse harem romance, omegaverse romance, and is branching out into contemporary romance. In her free time, she enjoys writing, reading, Dungeons & Dragons, table top games with her husband and friends, and playing with her son. M.P. also enjoys tv, movies, and music across various genres.

To get the most up-to-date information about her latest releases and book signings, check out www.mpstarkweather. com or follow her on your favorite social media site.

Also By M.P. Starkweather

Shared Worlds

- **A Horny Reindeer Story** <u>Mate Hunt: Dancer</u>

- **Monsters of New York (Evernight Publishing)** <u>Coyote Underground</u>

Standalones – Contemporary RH

<u>Finding Fiona</u>

Standalones - Contemporary RH OV

<u>Forsaken Omega</u> – free with newsletter signup

<u>Cold Princes</u>

<u>Knot My Valentine</u>

Omegas of Echo Falls – Contemporary RH OV Small Town
Series

<u>Hanna</u>
<u>Maisy</u>
<u>Karissa</u>

The Pack Next Door – Contemporary RH OV series

<u>Princess or Knot</u>

<u>Fiancée or Knot</u>

<u>Queen or Knot</u>

<u>The Pack Next Door: The Original Trilogy</u>

<u>Christmas or Knot</u>

Standalones – Paranormal RH

<u>The Wayward Girl</u>

The Cursed Blade Series – Paranormal w/ different pairings

Digital Blade – RH

Elemental Blade – RH

Vampires at Midnight - Paranormal RH series

Blood Moon

Blood Lost

Blood War

Vampires at Midnight: The Complete Trilogy

VaM/HoF Crossover Novella - Paranormal RH

Blood Wolf— free with newsletter signup

Hunters of the Forest - Paranormal RH series

Wolf Bane

Wolf Caged

Wolf Moon

Hunters of the Forest: The Complete Trilogy

Forged by Magic - Sci-fi/Fantasy M/F series

Hidden

Betrayed

Saved

Forged by Magic: The Complete Trilogy

Daydreams and Sunsets - a collection of poetry

Daydreams and Sunsets